PRAIS

Love the beach and Coastal Carolina? Consider reading the two series set in Emerald Isle, NC because ~ *It's always a good time for a love story and a trip to the beach!*

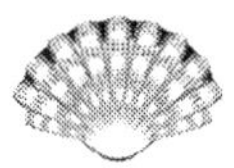

THE EMERALD ISLE, NC STORIES SERIES begins with the award-winning debut novel, *Beach Rental*, an RT Book Reviews TOP PICK. Here's what the reviewer wrote:

> "No author can come close to capturing the awe-inspiring essence of the North Carolina coast like Greene. Her debut novel seamlessly combines hope, love and faith, like the female equivalent of Nicholas Sparks. Her writing is meticulous and so finely detailed you'll hear the gulls overhead and the waves crashing onto shore. Grab a hanky, bury your toes in the sand and get ready to be swept away with this unforgettable beach read."

Or visit Emerald Isle, NC in the BAREFOOT TIDES SERIES that begins with *A Barefoot Tide*, in which a woman from the rural town of Cub Creek, Virginia accepts a temporary job that takes her to the beach—and discovers it may not be so easy to go home again.

Regarding Cub Creek, Virginia—a rural area *in the heart of Virginia, where the forests hide secrets and the creeks run strong and deep*—where Libbie (in *Cub Creek*) goes to hide from a world where she doesn't fit in…and finds her life. Or where Hannah (in *The Memory of Butterflies*) keeps a devastating secret to protect her loved ones. Or where Kara (in *Wildflower Heart*) finds healing from old wounds and heartbreak. Or where Jaynie (in *A Light Last Seen*) finds that you can—and often *should*—go home again.

A Light Last Seen* and *A Reader's View of Cub Creek

From a reader about Cub Creek and A Light Last Seen: "'In the heart of Virginia, where the forests hide secrets and the creeks run strong and deep,' is a place called Cub Creek. A place that has meadows filled with colorful flowers and butterflies to chase, and dirt roads and Cub Creek to jump over and disappear into the woods. A living and rural place that draws the reader to the setting and the characters who have stories to tell. A place with light and darkness and as unique as the characters who live there. When I opened the beautiful cover of this book, I stepped into the Cub Creek world and met the main character, Jaynie Highsmith. This is her story."—*Reader/Reviewer Bambi Rathman, February 2020*

WILDFLOWER WEDDING

A Wildflower House Novella

The Wildflower House Series, Book 4

Books by Grace Greene

Emerald Isle, North Carolina Series

Beach Rental *(Book 1)*

Beach Winds *(Book 2)*

Beach Wedding *(Book 3)*

"Beach Towel" (A Short Story)

Beach Walk *(Christmas Novella)*

Barefoot Tides Two-Book Series

A Barefoot Tide *(Book 1)*

A Dancing Tide *(Book 2)*

Beach Single-Title Novellas

Beach Christmas *(Christmas Novella)*

Clair *(Beach Brides Novella Series)*

Cub Creek Novels ~ Series and Single Titles

Cub Creek *(Cub Creek Series, Book 1)*

Leaving Cub Creek *(Cub Creek Series, Book 2)*

The Happiness In Between

The Memory of Butterflies

A Light Last Seen

The Wildflower House Novels

Wildflower Heart *(Book 1)*

Wildflower Hope *(Book 2)*

Wildflower Christmas *(A Wildflower House Novella) (Book 3)*

Wildflower Wedding *(A Wildflower House Novella) (Book 4)*

Virginia Country Roads

Kincaid's Hope

A Stranger in Wynnedower

www.GraceGreene.com

Brief Description

Wildflower Wedding (A Novella) is the fourth book in The Wildflower House Series by Grace Greene. Order of series: *Wildflower Heart, Wildflower Hope, Wildflower Christmas (A Novella), and Wildflower Wedding (A Novella).*

Wildflower Wedding ~ A love story that triumphs over past heartbreak to embrace new love, new hopes, maybe even a few miracles of the heart....

Kara is on track to turn the old mansion her father left her into a creative retreat and event space, but after a successful holiday season and then a joyous Christmas celebration with her friends and family, it's now January and winter has settled in. The brightest spot in the shorter, darker days, is the man she's fallen in love with. But she's worried. Suppose the growing relationship is more a distraction than a 'meant-to-be' love story. She has successfully stepped out on her own to drive the project she envisioned, but does she risk derailing her progress toward opening the Wildflower retreat in spring by taking another chance on love only to find heartbreak? Can her heart survive even the possibility of one more loss?

Wildflower Wedding

A Wildflower House Novella

The Wildflower House Series, Book 4

By Grace Greene

Kersey Creek Books

This is a work of fiction. Names, characters, organizations, places, events, and incidents are either products of the author's imagination or are used fictitiously. Any resemblance to actual persons, living or dead, or actual events is purely coincidental.

Published by Kersey Creek Books
Digital and print release – February 2022

ISBN-13: 978-1-7375486-9-0 (eBook)
ISBN-13: 978-1-7375486-8-3 (Print)
ISBN-13: 978-1-7375486-7-6 (Large Print)

Cover design by Grace Greene
Printed in the United States of America

Wildflower Wedding *is dedicated to*
snowy days and spring weddings
and to all the joys
found in ordinary ways and
small moments and big occasions
with those we love
and with whom we share our lives.
Endure what you must.
Seek out the good amid the chaos.
Celebrate that which uplifts you and
others.

Wildflower Wedding

Prologue

- *Wildflowers are tough. They root in unlikely, often hostile environments, yet they manage to grow and bloom.*
- *Wildflowers are fragile. Careless or deliberate acts can easily destroy them.*
- *Wildflowers grow where the seeds find themselves. They must succeed or perish. If they don't grow, no one notices. It's as if the seed or the flower never existed.*
- *Wildflowers are beautiful for a season. Some may be beautiful for seasons to come. The wildflower will never know the difference because it either is or isn't. Only the bees and the butterflies—or a human heart—may feel the lack.*

—Stitched by Kara Lange Hart at Wildflower House

The road that brought me to Wildflower House could easily be measured in miles. In fact, I'd done exactly that almost a year ago—the first time I'd traveled that stretch of I-64 and Route 522 to Cub Creek in Louisa County. Dad had just told me that he was retiring and moving to the country to a huge, decaying house in the middle of nowhere. He was planning to restore it, he'd said. Because I was living with him at the time, still recovering from the accident that had taken my husband and seriously injured me, he'd invited me to make the move too.

Frankly, I was stunned. Dad was sixty and healthy. He seemed much too young to retire, to give up the successful business he'd spent his life building. He'd have to learn the ins and outs of renovation. For that, his age would surely work against him. The whole idea didn't make sense to me. I suspected the real estate agent, a tall, slim blonde named Nicole, only a few years older than me, might be taking advantage of him.

But when I made the journey out to see the mansion that day and unexpectedly found myself in a field of wildflowers, in some strange and glorious way I was changed. Not miraculously healed, no, but finally able to believe that recovery was possible and perhaps even near.

I soon discovered I was wrong about Nicole, who became my friend, along with the people I met through her, including the rest of the Albers family.

So the road to Wildflower House could be measured in miles, but for me, it might be more appropriate to measure it in time. Not in the actual minutes and hours it took to travel those miles of asphalt, but by the life events that had gone before and those that came after. The time before included so much sadness—much of it caused by those around me. And while I lost my dad soon after we moved here, it also marked me taking control of my life and finally finding my own new road.

The road *I* chose.

I chose to move forward with the renovation of Wildflower House, to turn it into a creative retreat and event space. I saw my goal and moved toward it, step by step, hiring the appropriate artisans and craftsmen for the various tasks. And into this project plan of creativity and progress came Will Mercer. He arrived—with broad shoulders, dark hair, and blue eyes—to work as a gardener and landscaper. I hired him to tame the out-of-control growth of the neglected grounds and make them beautiful, but he also proved his skills beyond the greenery and became a necessary part of my life.

For me, over the course of late summer and into autumn, Wildflower House became a place of happiness. Of flowers. Of sweeping green lawns and healthy forests. It was a place to grow and continue growing, even as I gained unexpected friends, not to mention finding an aunt and uncle I'd never known about.

And I started to worry.

I was embarrassed to be feeling almost superstitious about Will's safety, as if ordinary things had become dangerous. But it is often a truth that the more important someone becomes to you, the more you fear losing them.

I'd often felt that the times of change in my life were beyond my control, driven by the decisions of others. Or by cruel fate. *Cruel* because bad things happened. *Cruel* also because good things happened—blessings and gifts—which were then inexplicably snatched away. After my father's sudden death in June, I'd chosen to take charge of my life and not to live subject to the whims of fate.

But that was easier said than done.

CHAPTER ONE

Late January ~

On any given day, the heart of Wildflower House might be found in its wide, high-ceilinged foyer, its gracious spaces, and in the century-old photograph of the girls and women hanging on the wall above the foyer table alongside my own needlework. The foyer seemed even larger because of the wide openings into the parlor on one side and the sitting room on the other. An upright piano was angled in a corner near the sitting room, and opposite it was the foyer table, though it looked more like a huge, dark chest with drawers than the foyer tables I was accustomed to seeing. The table and the piano had been among the furniture returned to Wildflower House by Sue Deale, the Forsters' heir, after my father, Henry Lange, had purchased the place last March.

Later, Dad and I would call this Wildflower House, but that first time I saw the empty house and unkempt grounds, I'd stumbled into the glorious field of wildflowers—a broad swath of bright color and humming life, bordered by thick woods on either side—and had heard the glorious music of Copland's *Appalachian Spring*, specifically the part that incorporated the old Shaker tune "Simple Gifts." It had taken me a few moments to realize the music was in me, in my head. I'd never tried to explain it to anyone else but had *simply*, gratefully, accepted the music as a *gift*.

I'd felt . . . renewed. Yes, perhaps that was the word, though it seemed inadequate to encompass the deep joy I'd experienced. It was a feeling of connectedness to the earth itself.

Thus, for a long time, I believed the sunlit gardens filling the open slope down to the creek and shady hideaway nooks in the edges of the forest were the life, the heart, of the property.

Dad and I had moved here in April. I'd told him that I would stay until the end of wildflower season, but then he'd died in June and left me abruptly and unexpectedly alone in that vast house in the country surrounded by forest.

For many months, it felt like Wildflower House and the property had lost its heart. *I* certainly had. Despite the support of the friends I'd made in Cub Creek, it was a struggle for me to get back on track—to commit to and pursue my goal of turning Wildflower House into a creative retreat and event space. Dad had told me I was resilient. Even my friend Mel Albers had called me that.

I did recover from my grief, but resuming life and *living* it are two different things. When I began *living* again, when happiness found me, it was because Will Mercer had come into my life.

I could hardly imagine the past months without him.

Last fall, when Sue Deale had asked to hold the book club meeting and then the Ladies' Auxiliary Holiday Open House here as our first, though unofficial, events, I had agreed. For the open house, Wildflower House was bedazzled with glitter and garland and fragrant fir boughs—all of which reflected in the deep grain of the warm wood paneling and the lustrous wood flooring. The grand stairway, with its wonderful carvings, seemed to speak of history, of lives lived—and my heart responded, coming fully alive for me again with the Christmas celebration I could never have planned—nor even have imagined—before these months at Wildflower House.

Hearts aside, and while I couldn't pin down exactly what made Wildflower House so special, I knew one thing for sure: when it came to human hearts, Will had mine. I was in love with him. He felt the same about me. We didn't use the actual word often—we were taking things slowly with our relationship—but it was evident in our every word and action.

In January, only weeks into the new year, I stood at the tall front windows, wearing a warm, oversized sweater hugged tightly around me against the chill. A deep cold had swept into the area right after the new year, and it had settled in. During that time, our biggest worry had been to keep the pipes from freezing. The furnace was working, but high ceilings and wide hallways—though lovely—were prone to drafts. Those drafts could be refreshing in warmer weather, but not in winter. And then, just as the temperatures rose a bit, snow entered the forecast.

The snow had started early that morning, then dwindled off, and now the flakes were no more than light, fluffy bits of white that danced in the gusty breeze and looked pretty, if cold. An inch or two covered the ground. It seemed to me that being in the country, as opposed to a city or subdivision with other signs of human life, the snow made me feel more isolated, as if the silent world within my reach was dormant, perhaps forever dormant. Empty. Almost like those days right after my father had died.

I hugged my sweater tighter. My mood was the fault of that dream—a stupid dream that had shaken me from sleep and driven me from my comfy bed, feather quilt, and soft pillows, afraid that if I *did* fall asleep again, the dream would return.

A dream should not be allowed to taint what would otherwise be a picture-postcard view of tall pines and a snow-covered landscape, with the small tracks of squirrels and deer the only marks in the snow, proving that other life did indeed exist.

Shake it off, Kara.

Standing there, watching, I was rewarded by seeing Will's truck come into view on the long driveway as he drove out of the wooded area between the house and the main road. This was my first time seeing the snowplow blade attached to the front of his truck. He'd warned me yesterday that if the forecast held, he'd be tied up all day and perhaps the next, clearing driveways and parking lots, along with salting and sanding—winter work he did for Mitchell's Lawn and Landscaping clients.

I hurried to the front door, even pushing wide the storm door, to greet him as he pulled to a stop in front of the house, but as he climbed from the truck and saw me leaning out, he waved me back inside.

"I'll be in shortly," he said.

I closed the storm door but stayed where I was, pulling my sweater more tightly around me, and watched him brush the loose snow from the steps and then toss sand on them.

He was dressed in a down jacket with a knit cap over his dark hair. His work boots were heavy-duty and meant for serious business.

Unexpectedly, a sudden chill struck through me. Scenes of slippery roads—especially winding, narrow country roads—of cars in ditches, of the myriad accidents that snow and ice can cause, slipped through my mind unbidden. I'd had no warning that those images, or the fears that came with them, were hiding in my brain and about to erupt.

That dream, I thought. It had planted that fear in me. In reflex, I opened the storm door again, probably to yell out *Be careful* or *Watch your step* or something equally foolish, and Will saw me.

"Kara?" He shouted louder, "Kara!"

I shivered with the cold and from those awful images and called back to him, "What? Can I help? Get you something?"

"Close that door. Keep the warmth in."

“Okay. Sure.” I tried to smile. “I’ll go fix you a thermos of coffee.”

“Thanks.”

I hurried down the long hallway to the kitchen. As I was heating the water and making the coffee, I realized he surely had his own battered thermos already filled for the day and on the passenger seat of his truck, along with whatever other items he wanted within easy reach while driving and working. No matter. He’d have this one too. And while I was fixing the coffee, I also bundled up some brownies and a peanut butter sandwich.

Will walked into the kitchen. He’d come silently up the hallway in his sock feet. He was wearing a flannel shirt and jeans but no coat, so he’d probably left it outside rather than risk dropping snow on my wooden floors.

“I hope you didn’t leave your coat out on the porch. It’s going to get that much colder.”

He smiled and peeked in the food bag. “Cold outside anyway. I’ll be in the truck most of the time. It’ll warm up quick.”

I stared at him, words and images bubbling in my brain.

“What’s wrong, Kara?”

I wouldn’t inflict my worries on him. I—

He moved around the table, closing the distance between us, but then he stopped short, only inches away, and spoke softly. “Tell me what’s on your mind. You aren’t yourself. I can see the worry.”

“You’ll laugh.”

“Never.”

Sighing, I said, “You could have an accident. Maybe run off the road into a ditch or . . . worse. You could be hurt.”

He slid his arms around me, pulling me close, and whispered in my ear, “I could be, but I won’t.” He tightened his hug as if in punctuation. “I could be hurt walking down those front steps, but I won’t be because I take precautions, like throwing down the sand. The risk of getting hurt is ever-present as a part of life.” He pulled away a fraction, still holding me, but now we were face-to-face. “I’m a professional, Kara. Might sound funny for a guy whose profession involves shovels—whether for earth or for snow—but I know the right precautions to take. I’ve been working for Jim Mitchell since I was a teenager. I have lots of experience”—he paused to press his lips to my throat—“with this type of work.” Then he stepped back abruptly, suddenly businesslike, but I saw the teasing in his unusually blue—perilous blue—eyes.

“Do you indeed?”

“Yes, and I know my job and my limits. I can’t stop you from worrying, but you are wasting your energy with that.” He brushed my cheek with his fingers. “I have so much to live for, to be healthy and in one piece for, that I won’t take chances.”

“Promise?”

“Promise.” He smoothed my hair back. “You have beautiful hair.”

“You’re changing the subject.” I tried to sound serious, but the breathy tone in my voice gave me away. Will’s distraction was working.

"It's just snowplowing, Kara. I can handle it. You haven't been worried when I was taking down trees with a chain saw or chasing snakes out of the brush with a rake. Why now?"

I shook my head, but awkwardly, refusing to mention the dream. To speak of it aloud would be like giving it power. A negative power that might even infect Will. I wanted him to have his mind on the work, not on my worries.

"I don't know, Will. I woke up feeling it. No good reason that I can think of . . . and that made me all the more anxious."

He grinned but said with a serious note in his voice, "Might be the change in the weather. People react to barometric changes more than they realize."

I frowned. "Seriously?"

He shrugged, but without releasing me, and so the movement had a funny, lighthearted feel to it.

"Interesting," I said. "I thought maybe I was worried about losing you because you are so very important to me." Now *I* grinned. "Nice to know it's probably just about a cold front moving in or out."

He lifted me right off my feet, set me on the counter, and then stood there, close to me, his hands on my knees.

"Say that again," he said.

I went blank for a moment, stunned by the intensity of his gaze—as if the future of the world itself hung on my response.

"Yes," I said. "What do you want me to say?" But I knew, and before he could answer, I pressed my fingers to his lips. "That you're important to me? You know that already. You know how I feel about you. You heard me say it to Seth just before Christmas."

His eyes went serious. "How long since we met?"

"Met? We met in June when you came with Jim Mitchell to discuss landscaping projects with Dad. Just before . . . just days before . . . we lost him."

"And when did we have our first conversation?"

"When you showed up in late July to work for me." Remembering the meeting warmed my insides. Made me feel all silly. Not because that meeting was brilliant, by any means, but it had been the first step that had led to the rest.

"So, seven months altogether."

"About that."

He nodded ever so slightly and sighed. "We need to talk."

For a long moment, I went silent. *Talk?* Not what I'd expected to hear.

"Talk," he said. "But not now, because I'm late and any moment now that phone is going to ring. Before it does . . ." He lifted me gently down but held me close.

"Talk about what, Will?"

He didn't answer. He kissed me instead. Until the phone rang.

He whispered, "Gotta go, Kara." In a quick motion, he answered the phone, saying "On my way" to whomever had called, then disconnected. He grabbed the lunch bag and thermos. "Depending on how the storm goes, I might be tied up all day, maybe all night. If there are trees down, it could be longer." He caught my gaze and said, "Don't worry. There are always a whole host of things to worry about today and into the future, but not this. Got it?"

"Yes." I believed him, and I sighed. "Yes."

"Don't wander outside unless you take your phone with you. If you slip and get hurt, no one will see you out here at Wildflower. Anything goes wrong? Call me. If you can't get me, call Mitchell's Landscaping. Libbie will know where to find me or Jim." He grinned once more. "She's an even bigger worrier than you are."

Then he was moving down the hall. I followed. As he approached the front door, he added, "We'll have to do some assessment about the drafts in this place. Can't eliminate them, but we can mitigate them."

Without Will holding me, I felt the cold more acutely. I pulled my sweater close around me again.

I stayed at the door, keeping it open a few inches while he tugged on his boots and shrugged into his coat. I refused to say *Be careful* and instead settled for, "Stay on the road, Will."

He said, "I'll do my best," as he pulled on his hat. With a deliberate pause and a serious expression on his face, he repeated, "We'll talk."

He descended the front steps and went to his truck.

Talk about what?

But he was already out of hearing. The truck moved slowly around the remaining circle of the drive and then headed out toward the road, vanishing into the trees and the snowflakes.

They were falling more heavily again.

Talk, he'd said. I mused silently about what he meant.

The view through the glass panel in the storm door was beautiful, but not the chill. This time, when I closed the door, I locked it. Will wouldn't be back for a while, and if anyone else chose to show up in a snowstorm, they'd need to knock.

Talk.

He'd probably said that just to give me a nothing-thing to worry over. A distraction. That would be Will's style—common sense with a dose of magic. I smiled.

Or maybe he'd been hinting . . .

No, I told myself. My heart rate increased along with a rising sense of panic. Will had been teasing me—a distraction that was well meant, but no more than that. I reminded myself that I had actual work to do, and if I was marooned here alone, there was no time like the present to get to it.

My project workroom was a plain, often-overlooked room along the main hallway. It was situated between the grand stairs and the narrow side hallway that led to the closeted servants' stairs and also out to a side porch and entryway. It was rarely used. As for the workroom, it might be plain, but it also had a door that could be closed, unlike those fancy front rooms, so it was perfect for use as an office.

We'd come a long way toward turning Wildflower House into a creative retreat and event space. The downstairs renovations were complete. Our unofficial events for the book club and the open house had been fun, done for goodwill, and were a great learning experience.

Hopefully, by late spring, we'd be ready to open for business in a real way, but there were many things yet to be done before that happened. For instance, work was in progress on the additional bathrooms upstairs. Nicole had recommended the plumber and carpenter, and both had warned me that if the snow arrived today, they and their crews might not.

Aunt Laura wasn't coming either. She drove over almost every day, but I didn't want her to risk driving in the snow, and she'd agreed.

So today would be a quiet day. I settled at the long table, opened my laptop, pulled up my project list, and went to work.

~~~~

Later that morning while I was in the kitchen, I heard merry voices—a woman laughing and a child squealing. I recognized that squeal.

Hurrying to the back door, I pushed the curtain aside. Five-year-old Maddie Lyn was tracking up the pristine layer of snow that stretched from the back of the house down to the creek.

I'd taken a few photos that morning, drawn by the unsullied scene. The snow had been a perfect blanket of white, and the creek banks, disappearing under the accumulation, had made the dark, flowing water seem the only living thing in the suspended landscape. But Maddie and her aunt Nicole were changing the pastoral, slightly mysterious-looking scene into a playground. When
~~~~

Maddie dropped onto her back and started swinging her arms and legs to make a snow angel, I wasn't surprised, but when Nicole joined her, I was flabbergasted.

Nicole. The ever-dignified, business-only Nicole. Making snow angels. *Good for her.* I'd never made one. But then, my childhood had been a little different than most.

I opened the back door. The porch and steps had maybe three inches of snow on them despite being somewhat sheltered by the porch roof. Slippery, surely. I called out, "When you get cold, join me for hot cocoa?"

Nicole sat up and waved, but Maddie called out from her prone position, "Okay! With marshmallows!"

"Will do. I'll get the cocoa heating up."

After a few minutes, I heard them on the back steps and looked out. Nicole had a tight grip on Maddie Lyn's arm and what looked like a death grip on the handrailing.

"Is it very slippery?"

"Not too much. Not as slippery as this little girl."

Maddie laughed, and when they reached the porch, she stomped her boots mightily to shake the loose snow from them.

I pulled Maddie into the house, and right there on the kitchen linoleum, I helped her out of her hooded jacket, her knitted cap and scarf, gloves, and the snow pants, until she was stripped down to her corduroy pants and a ruffly shirt with appliqued butterflies. Her hair clung to her scalp and the side of her face. Her cheeks were rosy red, and her eyes were bright with excitement.

"*Snow*, Aunt Kara. *It snowed.*"

I laughed. "I noticed." I glanced at Nicole, who'd removed her own gloves, jacket, and hat and was now walking to the counter where I had the mugs lined up. She brought the mugs to the table, plus the bowl of tiny marshmallows with them.

Nicole said, "We came to see how you're doing in this winter wonderland all alone." She gave me a look. "I presume you *are* alone?"

"Laura didn't attempt the drive. I encouraged her to stay home. She's been here almost every day, learning how to enter receipts into the spreadsheet and such things. She wants to be helpful, and I hope we can work out something permanent. Something related to the business, you know?"

Nicole nodded and sipped her cocoa before saying, "I may have some suggestions. We'll talk, if you'd like, but not today." She drained the last sip chocolate with audible satisfaction and grinned at Maddie Lyn. "Not today because Maddie and I are going home to build a snowman."

"The best snowman ever," Maddie added.

"We'll build it where Grammy can look out and watch."

"Yup," she said.

She had a cocoa mustache on her upper lip. I resisted the urge to wipe it off, but I couldn't help but smile.

Nicole said, "You're welcome to join us, Aunt Kara."

I was tempted to go with them but wouldn't. I laughed, saying, "Thanks, but I need to buy taller boots before I venture out there. That snow's still coming down."

Nicole gave me a long look. Her expression was bland, but in her eyes I could see the calculations running. Apparently, she decided all was well, or well enough, because she said, "Maddie Lyn, let's get you suited back up."

I went to retrieve the snow gear she'd arrived in from where we'd spread it all out on the floor. I said, "It was kind of you to come check on me."

She smiled. "It was the perfect walk on a snowy day." In a lower, more casual tone, she asked, "You aren't too lonely? Is Will coming by?"

"Maybe, but he'll probably be too busy since the storm doesn't seem to be letting up."

"You want to be here if he does."

It wasn't stated as a question, and wasn't her business anyway, so I didn't answer. I glanced up, though, and saw a small smile on her lips.

She said, "Keep your cell phone handy and charged. Call if you need us."

"Thanks, Nicole."

"Remember, Mom has a generator, so if you lose power, come on over."

Maddie was once again done up like a winter sausage. She said, "Let's go. I'm hot."

"Good," I said. "Stay that way—warm—and have fun."

They left.

Funny how simple things like a child's laughter and a friend's good will could color the day brightly and warm up one's attitude. After Nicole and Maddie left to make their way home through the snow, the brightness and warmth stayed with me. I felt less isolated, even though I was, in fact, as alone as before.

Simple things made the difference, I thought. They were much like small, unexpected gifts.

Instead of returning to the workroom, I found myself in the foyer, standing in front of the piano.

"Simple Gifts" and *Appalachian Spring* tuned up in my head.

I'd heard music that day in late March almost a year ago when I'd first seen this place and had discovered the field of wildflowers. It had played in my head—through my poor brain that I'd believed was still suffering from the effects of the automobile accident—as if I were a receiver of some kind. I'd been lost, gladly so, in the sight, sound, and scents of the flowers and music. Later, after Dad died, Victoria had surprised me by playing that same tune on this piano. Then Will . . . he'd surprised me by the strength, the force, of his own playing—but playing music I hadn't recognized before turning his attention to gentler Christmas carols for Maddie Lyn.

I raised the lid and felt it slide easily back into the cabinet. I touched the keys with a tentative pling and then another pling, much as Maddie had done when she'd tested the piano herself months ago. Fingers—those of the people I cared about and of others unknown to me—had touched these same ivory keys.

Sitting on the bench, I thought of the women in the picture on the wall behind me. This instrument hadn't been *their* piano. It had belonged to the Forsters, the couple who'd lived here at Wildflower before us. When they'd died, Sue Deale, their heir, had taken it, along with the entire contents of the house, much to her husband's dismay. After Dad and I had moved in, she'd returned some of the furniture, no doubt at the urging of her husband. But at the turn of the prior century, surely any self-respecting girls' school had had a piano. Probably one very similar to this one. The sounds of a piano filling these rooms would not be unfamiliar here.

Too bad I didn't know how to play.

I ran my fingers over the smooth wooden cabinet and then back down to the keys, where I swept my fingers along the length of them, actually hearing a couple of keys that gave me pause. I might not know how to play, but my ears worked, and this piano needed tuning.

Instead of working on project plans and budgets and promotional materials, or list after list of things to do, I sat on the piano bench and thought of Nicole and the look she'd given me when she'd invited me to go play in the snow with her and Maddie. I'd claimed not to have tall enough boots. She'd asked whether I was staying home because Will might drop by, but her look had asked more.

It wasn't long ago that I'd thought I was falling in love with her brother, Seth. She knew there was no future for me and Seth, that Will and I had become a couple. She was surely asking, albeit unspoken, how that relationship was progressing. And because she was a businesswoman through and through, she was actually asking what a relationship with Will might mean to my plans for Wildflower House.

I appreciated Nicole's help. She'd been incredibly helpful to me with building the business and as a friend, because, yes, I considered her my friend. But I wasn't going to open my heart up for her calculation and assessment. I hit one of the lower, deeper keys solidly to underscore that thought. I was a private person. As my father and mother had been too. And I had a right to that privacy. Love, worries, fears—the whole tangled yarn ball of my life—was for me to share or not, as I chose.

I laughed at that mental image. Mine would be a very colorful yarn ball indeed. I thought of my embroidery threads and couldn't help glancing behind me at my needlework hanging above the foyer table next to the photograph of the women. I'd stitched that piece about the wildflowers during the dark time after my father died. I did very little stitching these days. Embroidery had gotten me through some very rough times. It had been a source of calm during confusion. Maybe when things were settled and the retreat was up and running, I'd have time to start a new needlework project.

But for now, I was here and waiting, in case Will showed up. I knew he was busy with the snow, and yet if he found a moment to drop by, I wanted to be here.

I hit a few keys, trying to remember what little I'd known about reading music.

What was that old phrase? Tickling the ivories? For me, it was more like *plinking the keys*. No matter. I made a mental note to find a piano tuner. Maybe then I'd be able to persuade Will to play for me. I'd mentioned it to him once or twice in a passing way since Christmas, but he hadn't taken the hint.

And then, in my procrastinating musings, I heard a truck and a rougher sound that made me think of snow removal. I rushed to the window. Will's truck. My heart responded. He was shaving off the top inches of snow from my graveled drive. At least I could now distinguish the driveway area from the grounds on either side of it.

I turned on the foyer lights and opened the door wide, to make sure Will knew that he was expected . . . and wanted.

~~~~

"I can't stay," he said as he kicked off his work boots before stepping inside.

I unwound the scarf from his neck as he pulled off his cap. His thick, dark hair was all awry, and without thinking I reached up to comb it with my fingers.

He'd removed his gloves too, and I felt the warmth of his flesh as he touched my neck.

"How's it going?" I asked.

"Easy snow, so far. No ice, but it's a wetter, heavier snow falling now, and the wind is expected to pick up. Could bring down some trees or lines. Do you want a ride into town? It'll get cold fast in this house if you lose power."

"It's snow, Will. I'm not out in it. I'm safe here." I remembered what Nicole had said. "If the power goes out, I'll wrap up and go over to Mel's. She has a generator."

"Call me first. A normally easy walk can be different
~~~~

if things ice up. Make sure you fully charge your phone, and if the power goes, call me."

"I will."

He nodded.

"Can I get you something to eat? Maybe soup or a sandwich? More coffee?"

"No more coffee," he laughed. "How about a tall glass of that fruit water you make?"

He waited in the foyer, and I hurried to find a large water bottle, found two instead, and filled them both with the fruit water. I snagged the box of cookies and took that to him too.

He was staring at the piano, at the open lid and the exposed keys.

"Were you playing?" he asked.

"What I was doing can't be considered playing." There was a long silence, and I added, "I'm hoping you'll play it for me again. Not carols, but whatever you like best to play." I kind of trailed off. Lamely, I added, "I'm going to get it properly tuned."

He left the foyer rug and came to where I stood, still holding the water bottles and cookies, now crushed between us as he held me. So many scents overwhelmed me. Hours he'd spent working in his truck, yes, but I could also smell the earth, the snow, the wintry air, the coffee, even truck exhaust, which made me think of the tedium of long, slow hours of clearing the things people built and needed available to make their lives work better. And the people like him who did the work to make that happen.

"Is that hug for the water or the promise of a piano

tuner?"

"For everything. Stay inside. Call me if you need me."

"Thank you, Will," I said. "And if you need a place to rest, I'll be here."

He looked . . . I didn't know. His expression was unreadable.

His rough cheeks scratched mine as he hugged me again, and then the bottles and cookies were in *his* arms, and he was gone.

~~~~

The wind did pick up, and shortly before midnight, Will returned. This time he brought Aunt Laura. He'd called on the way. She'd lost power.

I checked the guest rooms. Only one was largely undisturbed by the renovation work. I tidied that room and put fresh sheets on the bed, looking forward to having her at the house with me tonight and in the morning.

Sometimes it was nice to have a friendly face around.
~~~~

Chapter Two

Early February ~

Laura had come to stay overnight because she'd lost power in the storm. She'd gone home as soon as the roads were clear enough, but found her power was still out, so she'd gathered additional toiletries and fresh clothing and returned to Wildflower for a few more days. We were now into the first days of February. When she got the call saying her power was restored, she left again. With thanks, of course, because we enjoyed each other's company, but everyone loves their particular creature comforts. I knew she was glad to be home and in her own space.

I was happy for her, and I understood. I didn't mind having time alone either. About lunchtime, I was in the kitchen making a snack to take back to the project workroom with me, when Victoria's voice echoed up the hallway.

"Hello? Kara? It's me!"

Slightly annoyed, I left the kitchen to greet her. I'd locked the front door, hadn't I? At the very least, I'd locked the storm door. Not that I minded seeing Victoria, but I did mind the interruption and the energy that would roll in with her like a bulldozer.

"I'm here," I called out, adding, "I wasn't expecting you," as I reached her.

"It's a surprise." She smiled. "I had the afternoon off and decided it was a beautiful day for a drive. The snow is almost all melted. I fancy there's even a hint of spring in the air."

"Wishful thinking. We're barely into February."

She shrugged. "Still a lovely day for a drive. Plus, I wanted to see how the upstairs bathrooms turned out. Are they finished?"

"Mostly done." I gestured toward the kitchen. "Would you like something to drink? I just made tea."

"Tea, huh?"

"Will enjoys sweet iced tea. I try to keep some fresh for him."

"Is he here?" She was looking around as if he might be hiding nearby.

"No, he's working a job. Some sort of muddy reclamation project. I don't know exactly what, but it's taking a lot of his time." I shrugged. "Come on up and see the progress for yourself."

I'd had an adjoining bathroom added between the right front bedroom and the room just behind it that overlooked the side of the house. I'd also had a nicer bathroom added to the room on the left, the largest bedroom, the room that had been my father's. It would be the best accommodation I could offer to overnight guests.

"Very nice," she said as she examined the new

bathrooms in detail. In the largest, she paused to observe her own face and hair in the mirror and smooth her curls before turning back to me. “You should move into this room. Take advantage of this lovely bathroom.”

I frowned. “I’m happy with my room at the back.”

“You liked that bedroom because of the wildflower view. That’s what you said. But the flowers are gone now.”

“Not forever. We’ll still have areas of wildflowers come spring. But there’s more to it than that. I love the openness of the view and the creek and so on. While the hall bath isn’t as private, I enjoy that old claw-foot tub, so I’m content.”

“Suit yourself, I suppose.” She added, “It’s looking good. Do you have any events or classes set up yet?”

“Not yet. I have instructors lined up. Hannah Cooper has agreed to teach clay work and pottery, and Nicole has someone who’d like to hold yoga classes on the lawn . . . that sort of thing. I’m working on getting the details down and deciding on graphics and all that. When we have the brochures and marketing materials ready to go, hopefully, the rest will be ready too.”

“Hopefully?”

“Hopefully. It’s a lot of moving parts, Vic. It’ll come together. We wouldn’t be expecting activities and customers and such during the winter. Maybe *next* winter if we have established teachers and clientele. For now, I’m targeting spring. Maybe late April or May for the first class or retreat offering.” I added, “If anyone is even interested in coming at all.”

Victoria laughed. "We have to work on your optimism, my friend." As we walked back down the stairs, she said, "What's all this *we* stuff anyway? *We* expect . . . *we* hope . . . *we* this and that. Is it the royal *we*? Or do you have actual partners now?"

"It's no different than before. Friendly partners assisting me. Nicole, of course, and others as I need them. I'm very fortunate."

"And?"

I shook my head. "And what?"

"Not what, but *who. Him. Will.* I thought *he* might be figuring into the *we*."

"Oh." I sighed, despite myself. "Yes. Without Will I can't imagine doing any of this." I stopped and leaned against the newel post, saying, "Or rather, I'd still be doing it, but it wouldn't be nearly as much fun. Plus, he has such great ideas and a lot of the skills needed to make them happen. He gives the ideas life."

Victoria smiled. "How's that going to work after the place opens for business? For the two of you?"

I shrugged. "No differently."

"Okay," she said, but her tone was noncommittal.

We walked to the kitchen, and I poured us each a glass of fruit water. "Pound cake or cookies?"

"Pound cake."

I sliced us each a piece and joined her at the table.

Between bites, she asked, "What did you get Will for Valentine's Day?"

I froze.

She said slowly, "It's almost Valentine's Day, Kara."

"Of course," I said. "I bought him a card."

She peered at me, looking almost suspicious. "A card . . . You don't have something—or maybe *planning* even a *little* something special—for Will?" When I didn't answer, she shook her head impatiently. "Kara, I can all but *guarantee* he's got something special in mind for you."

Of course he did. And by forcing the issue, she was tapping straight into my worries—poking at my fears—a little *too* on point. I frowned, saying harshly, "We'll go out to eat. I'll find a special place to suggest."

"Seriously?" She gave me a dispirited gaze. "Honestly, Kara, Will is not just in love with you . . . he'd follow you to the ends of the earth and back on your merest whim. He's devoted to you. *Everyone* can see his heart is totally at your disposal." She dropped her voice to a softer tone, adding, "I'm guessing he isn't the kind of guy who falls in love on a whim. This is serious for him. Am I wrong?"

I shrugged and got up from the table.

Victoria insisted, "And you feel the same. You may not realize how obvious it is to everyone, but those who see the two of you together can't miss it. So what's the problem? What's wrong?"

That lesser, negative, defensive part of my personality jerked me back into past grievances with Victoria and whispered in my head, and I spun around to confront her. "Do you have any particular reason to think he has . . . big plans? Have you been talking to him?"

Her face went blank, which, when it came to Victoria,

was alarming and reminded me that I'd already forgiven her for her past lapses in being a good friend. I should never have suggested she'd spoken with Will behind my back, especially since it was done solely to shut her up. She was right about Will. I went over to her and put my hand on hers.

"I'm sorry, Vic. I'm anxious. I have been for several weeks." Admitting it aloud—my weakness—felt shameful. "I have so much to be grateful for. Only a fool finds things to worry about instead of enjoying the good. Every time I think I'm okay again . . ."

"Kara," she whispered, "not everything in life makes sense. Least of all where the human heart is involved." She took my hand, saying, "It will be okay. Seems like you're borrowing trouble again. You and Will were so good together over Christmas. Did something happen?"

"Will's been great. But . . . I don't know how to explain my nerves except that I feel as if a big change is about to happen. That fate is about to screw with my life again." I tried to breathe. "I can't lose anyone else. I simply can't."

"But, Kara . . . suppose that the big change is a good one? Suppose . . ."

But I couldn't listen to more. I had to move. I walked away, draining the last of the water in my glass and pretending I was thirsty and going to the fridge for more.

Victoria tried again, asking, "What set you off? Something must've."

I took a long drink of fruit water, then held my eyes closed and breathed slowly.

"Kara . . ."

"It was that dream."

"What dream?"

"Just a stupid dream that keeps coming back. The first time was when Dad and I were moving in here. In the dream, I was in this house. The floors were gleaming, and the rooms were empty of furniture and seemed endless, and I was dancing—or rather, standing there in a long white dress and waiting to dance when a man walked in. Seth. I tried to take his hand but couldn't, and then he stepped away, like vanishing, and another man was in the corner. I knew it was Niles, and even though I couldn't make out his features, I knew he was watching and blaming me for the accident that claimed his life."

I rubbed my temples and felt the ghost of the scar in my hairline.

"Then the dream ended, and soon after that Seth and I went our own ways. And that was it. The dream didn't return until last month, during the night before the snow. This time, the man who walked into the room was Will. Clearly Will. Unmistakably Will." I shocked myself, ending the sentence practically in a sob.

Victoria rushed over to me. She put her hands on my arms. Her smile was huge. "But don't you see? It *is* a good news dream. That *dream* man was Will. And now, you and he—"

I interrupted. "It was Will, yes, but instead of dancing with me, he vanished too. As if . . . as if he'd been swallowed by darkness, by the very floor beneath our feet. As if Wildflower House itself had taken him from me."

Now I was shaking.

Victoria put her arms around me and hugged. "It's all good, Kara. It will take a whole lot more than some weird dream to run Will Mercer off."

She stepped back just enough to talk to me face-to-face. "He's tough, Kara. He's tough in a way that has staying power, unless you, yourself, run him off. And while you might be nuts sometimes, you aren't crazy."

When I didn't respond, she shook me a little. "Kara, please laugh. Smile a little. Don't cheat yourself out of happiness just because things are beginning to feel out of your control."

"Is that it, Vic?"

She nodded. "Seems likely. You tend to go on the defensive-offensive when that happens. That dream—"

"It felt like a warning. Like I should . . . take heed. But I couldn't say any of that to Will."

"No, and you shouldn't. He may think you secretly *do* want him to go but don't want to say it." She shook her head. "It was only a dream. Rather, a nightmare, maybe. It could've been caused by something you ate. It could be pointless guilt over past events—which it shouldn't be, because there's no guilt on you for what happened to Niles. As for Seth . . . you two wanted—still want—different things."

Like Niles, I thought, though Victoria left that unsaid. Niles and I had loved each other once upon a time, but had we ever *known* each other? Or had we just seen what we wanted to see, and when finally we did see the truth, we didn't like it? Maybe. Niles had been Victoria's friend too, and she hadn't paused in the slightest when she'd said I shouldn't feel guilty for his death. She didn't blame me, even though I'd been the driver.

"No guilt?" I asked.

"No. A thousand times *no*. Don't cheat yourself of happiness."

"You're right, I shouldn't." This moment felt almost like a dream state itself. I was tempted to pinch myself, except that this was Victoria I was talking to, and she was too alive to be confined to a dream story.

"That's better. Good to see a smile on your face." She released me and turned back toward the table, but then she stopped abruptly, swinging back around to face me, her eyes wide. "Do you think he . . . That Will might be . . . Do you think it's because he's getting so serious, that he's planning to propose? Is that what's freaking you out? Commitment?" She laughed and clapped her hands. "That's it, isn't it?"

"Propose? *No*. He understands I need to take this slowly, to let our relationship grow."

She squinted and tilted her head. "You've been growing this relationship for *months* already."

"For only a *few* months."

"Kara. You two can hardly keep your hands off each other."

"Are we that annoying? I'm sorry." My face was hot. *No blushing,* I told myself as I pressed my hands together. "Enough for now. Thank you for the support and good advice. You are right that I need to do something special for Valentine's Day. I knew that. I was procrastinating, I guess."

"Not procrastinating. Avoiding."

"Enough, Vic. I get your point."

She opened her mouth to speak. She wanted to say more. But instead, she drew in a deep breath, gave me a smile, and said, "So, it's looking good around here. Need my help with anything else?"

CHAPTER THREE

A week before Valentine's Day ~

Victoria had helped clear my head and focus my thoughts by throwing a big bucket of common sense all over me. Not that my anxiety was cured—that would be magical indeed—but I was letting optimism have the upper hand. Will had not mentioned having that *talk* again, nor had he proposed. I loved him and hoped marriage was in our future, but I was glad not to be put to the test right now. It was too soon for that. There were too many unknowns. I knew he wanted more. From me. With me. And each time those thoughts intruded, they mixed with lesser feelings, worries left from darker times, and I felt scared.

Victoria was right. That's where the dream had come from. I disregarded the dream now. Each time anxiety edged in, I borrowed a bit more of Victoria's common sense, reminding myself that there were valid reasons to worry—my history, for one thing—but history was history, and I couldn't change it.

Will knew a lot of it. He understood my restraint. He was almost two years younger than me, had never been married, and while I knew he'd had a breakup or two in his life, it wasn't the same as my own disastrous marriage and the auto accident that had taken my husband and badly injured me. My limp was gone, but there were still scars on my legs from the accident, plus invisible scars that showed up uninvited.

Will was the only one who could decide if he was able to deal with all that. Rushing into commitment would only lead us down the paths I'd traveled before with Niles and Seth.

Will drove all over the area for the various jobs he worked for Mitchell's Lawn and Landscaping. This time of year, most of that work was done in cold, messy weather. He stopped by when he could, and often for a meal. A few days after Victoria's visit, and with her words still ringing in my ears, I brought up the subject of Valentine's Day. Together, Will and I decided we'd go somewhere special. Will joked that he'd bring along a fancy box of chocolates. I laughed and promised to share them with him. It felt really good to me to confirm that we were on the same page relationship-wise. And if Will seemed subdued or distracted over the next week or so . . . well, I could hardly blame him. He worked very hard.

The dream didn't return. I focused on the jobs at hand—finalizing the marketing materials for Wildflower House, among so many other tasks, including helping Aunt Laura learn the computer and how to work with spreadsheets.

CHAPTER FOUR

Valentine's Day ~

On Valentine's Day, Aunt Laura was in the workroom, entering receipts into the spreadsheet. She wasn't comfortable with the computer and often pressed the wrong key, and then we'd have to spend time undoing the error, all the while with Laura apologizing. I told her it was all good. No worries. But it did fray my nerves a bit, so when Will showed up just after lunch, I was delighted to see him.

I would've been delighted anyway.

Leaving Laura in the workroom, I drew Will back to the kitchen, where I welcomed him properly. After a short while, I asked, "Can you stay for lunch? I can rustle up something pretty quickly."

"Can't. I'm tasked with job estimates today. After the storm, and with spring just over a month away, our schedule will fill up fast." He downed a glass of iced tea in nothing flat, then set the glass on the counter. "Nice. You've gotten good at making sweet tea. I detected something more in it, though. Was that strawberry?"

"Too much?"

"No. It's a faint flavor. A hint. I like it."

Smiling, I stretched to kiss his cheek.

"The schedule." He kept his arm around me. "It's filling up. I said that, right? I was thinking about what we discussed—clearing the Lange property."

That chill was back. The sharp edge of anxiety was trying to find a way back in. *Don't be stupid,* I told myself. *I want the land cleared, right?*

"Yes."

Will heard the lack of enthusiasm in my tone.

"Have you changed your mind?" He touched my hair. "When we discussed it back in . . . November or December? You seemed certain then. Regardless, we were concerned about liability, right? Someone could wander into that mess. Not only unsightly, but it's an unnecessary risk."

I nodded. "I guess it fell off my radar, so to speak. I've been busy trying to get things pulled together here for the business."

"The business was part of the reason for clearing it."

"We discussed doing it in the spring, didn't we? When the ground is firmer for the equipment you'll need, but the trees haven't leafed out and the sticker bushes aren't so thick? For better visibility, right?"

"Exactly. But we should get it on the Mitchell's Lawn and Landscaping schedule now."

Pushing away ever so slightly, I said, "Of course."

He frowned. I saw his puzzlement and tried to sound more enthusiastic.

"So when do you think it will happen? How long will it take?"

He shrugged. "Once we're in there, the dismantling and hauling won't take more than a day or two. The tricky part is improving that old road so we can get the equipment back there, and then after the debris is removed we can see what needs to be dealt with. Like the well, for instance. We can't be sure what's under the debris, or under the leaves and downed branches. Not safe to poke around in that mess. Better to use the equipment to clear off the big stuff on top first."

"I see." Worry tried to overwhelm me. I shook it off. "Whatever you think best, Will. You're the expert." I gave in to the worry just a bit by adding, "Be careful, okay?"

"Always am," he said. "I have too much to lose." He touched my hair. "Any new thoughts on what you want to do with the property after it's cleared?"

I shook my head. "No. I'll wait until after it's done and see if inspiration strikes."

Will said, "Are we still on for supper?"

"Yes, unless something has come up for you? I know you're busy."

He laughed softly. "Not a chance. Today is special."

"Valentine's Day?"

"*Our* Valentine's Day."

Ours. Our *first*.

I asked, "Where shall we go? You said it was a surprise. What time should I be ready?"

"Actually, I hope you won't mind. I did make a reservation, but I canceled it because the restaurants are going to be packed. Do you mind if we eat here? I'll bring something with me."

"I don't mind at all. I can cook."

"So can I," he said, "but let's keep it simple. Takeout."

"Okay."

"Do you have a preference?"

"Not really. I'll fix a salad to go along with whatever you choose to surprise me with."

He pressed a quick kiss to my forehead. "A surprise. Do you like surprises, Kara?"

"Depends on the surprise, I think." I laughed. Actually, I didn't like surprises much at all, but I was pretty sure I could handle whatever takeout Will *surprised* me with. We had some good food options within the larger area of Mineral and Louisa, but nothing too far out of the ordinary.

Will left soon after, and then Laura said she had errands to run before heading home, gave me a hug, and left too.

As soon as she was gone, I finished up what we'd been working on, tidied the work area, and then went upstairs to tidy myself and decide what to wear for our Valentine's dinner. I didn't know exactly what time Will would show up. I'd learned over our time together that he might or might not call to let me know. Just as he didn't always answer his phone. Sometimes he even left it in his truck. We had that in common—not feeling tied to the phone or to email. Will was competent with electronics, but he was at his best with green growing things, or shaping the landscape, or even reclaiming and restoring the landscape. Plus, he'd built the bookcase in the parlor. It seemed to me he was, at heart, an artist. The work he did, both outside and in, was crafted with skill and talent. He was generally a very low-key dresser, usually wearing jeans and a T-shirt, and I wouldn't want to make him feel underdressed by overdoing it this evening.

My brain was whirling as if this was a major occasion, but I was enjoying myself, anticipating his return. It had been a long time since I'd given this much thought to which earrings to wear or to choosing a shade of lipstick.

This evening was special, as Victoria had insisted. And Will was a romantic, as I was discovering.

Mauve rose, I decided. Understated, but inviting.

~~~~

Will and I usually ate in the kitchen—it was friendly and companionable—but this was Valentine's Day. Will saw tonight as special. I did too. The dining room with its huge table and formal décor and the chandelier above was over-the-top, maybe . . . but why not?

I set the table with the nicer dishes and glasses and even put out candles in crystal holders. When I was satisfied, I clapped my hands in delight, knowing this would please Will, and then I flipped the light switch off and went to the kitchen to prepare the salad.

Will texted that he was on the way.

Perfect timing, I wrote back. *What are you bringing?*

A surprise.
~~~~

Such a simple word. Yet it could encompass so much—anything from chicken to burgers to sushi. I laughed.

A short time later, I heard his truck and went to the front door.

He parked in the circular drive near the porch, and when he climbed out of his truck, the first thing I noticed was that he'd changed his clothing too. For takeout? Maybe the estimating job had been messier than he'd expected? And not just changed, but he was wearing a white dress shirt that was crisply ironed. Professionally pressed, by the looks of it. And his boots had been replaced by shined loafers. He smiled broadly as he moved from the truck to the porch, lifting the brown bags of food high like trophies.

He was still smiling as he entered the house and gave me a quick kiss. Even as we emptied the food from the bags and carried the plates to the dining room, he was clearly pleased—but every so often his smile would slip and I glimpsed an unexpected, unaccustomed undertone. A somber look. Did Will have something on his mind?

We sat together at the table, but I stopped him before we started eating.

"Will, is there a problem?"

"No, not a problem. Why?" But he looked sheepish.

"You seem preoccupied. Want to talk?"

I expected a *no*, but instead, he set his fork down and said, "Yes, there is something. I was going to bring it up later, after we ate, but"—he flashed that quick, rueful half smile and then looked away—"I've been wanting to talk to you about this, and I kept talking *myself* out of it. A few days ago, I decided *now* is the time."

Uneasy, I waited.

He stared down at the table and then slowly, deliberately, he looked at me, face-to-face. His eyes—those striking eyes—met mine as he said, "I mislead you earlier. I canceled the dinner reservations, yes, but not simply because the restaurants were crowded—you know I'm proud to be seen with you anywhere and everywhere—but there would be people in town who'd recognize us, and for this, I thought it was better to be private. I didn't want to put you on the spot . . . when I ask you to marry me, Kara."

He sat back, his fingers impatiently raking his hair back from his forehead. He shook his head. "I'd planned it all out in my mind, exactly what and how to say it. Taking a knee, all the right words . . . Sorry. I've never proposed before, but I hope my sincerity will speak for me, will make up for my lack of style."

His eyes stayed on my face. My expression felt wooden. I felt stunned, almost paralyzed.

He continued, "Hear me out, Kara. I've thought this through. I knew your first impulse would be to say no and run. I understand you may not be ready to make a commitment, but think on it. I'm not interested in dating anyone else. I'm not the kind of guy who does important things like this on a whim, though"—he gave a quick grimace—"you are even *less* impulsive than I am. I expect you'll want to discuss it when you're over the first surprise . . ." He touched my hand. "I *want* you to think about it, if you need to." He didn't hold my hand, but merely rested his fingers, warm and strong, upon mine.

"But how surprised are you, really, Kara?"

"Will . . ."

"I know you love me. I've heard you say it, remember? Just this past Christmas. I don't think you've changed your mind, because I see your smile when you see me, I've held you and kissed you. I may know your moods better than you do. I'm looking forward to finding out what I don't know about you. I think we can do amazing things together. There are, however, reasons why you might not want to commit to me."

He nodded as if to confirm what he was saying. "Economic reasons. Job reasons. I'm a gardener, a landscaper, a handyman—and I'm happy that way. I'm always ready to help you in any way you need, but I have no greater ambition than being as I am. You may have other reasons to hesitate that I'm not aware of, but it feels to me that we should take this next step. Get out of this gray area of commitment without commitment. We need to be honest with each other, and this is my honesty—this is what I want. I want to marry you."

He stood, this time holding my hand and keeping it in his, so I stood with him.

"Kara, don't answer me this evening unless you want to." He paused. When I didn't speak, he said softly, "Take a few days to think about it, and then we'll have this conversation again."

Oh, elusive words. Poor, fickle constructs for critical, life-changing events—words were inadequate and unreliable when they truly mattered. They whirled in my brain. I tried to catch the right ones—to sort them out from the morass of surprise and fear and worry and desire. And while I was staring and sorting, Will tried to be patient and hopeful. It was all plainly written across his face.

He released my hand and put his arms around me, slowly and carefully, as if fearing I might try to break away. I wanted to run. Away from his arms and into them at the same time, and for those few moments that seemed to stretch into forever, the conflict did truly paralyze me.

He touched my face, my throat, saying, "Maybe I rushed it. But this—doing it now—felt important, Kara. As if . . . time mattered."

It does matter, my heart cried. Oh, time did matter, but we—Will and I—mattered more. Inconvenient or not. Ready or not. Time got shorter every day. But rushing—making poor choices—could also wreck what might be good if allowed to grow.

"Will . . ."

He said, "Don't. Please. Don't say no yet. Give it some thought."

I nodded.

"Promise?"

"I promise."

He leaned toward me and pressed his lips to mine. So lightly. Too lightly. When he pulled away, I followed instinctively, leaning toward him. And I saw the truth in his eyes—that he'd wanted me to say yes immediately, despite what he'd said. To say yes and throw my arms around him and shout my happiness.

I gasped as he released me and reached for his jacket. "Will—"

"I should go. Don't be angry, please." He added, "Remember, you promised to think about it." And with that, he walked out the front door, closing it carefully behind him.

He left?

Seriously?

I was stunned, but only for a moment, and then, startling even myself, I ran to the door, shouting after him, "Yes." But it was too late. He was already driving away.

Standing on the porch, shivering in the February evening, I watched the truck taillights grow small and then disappear into the trees. Still, I waited, thinking he might realize how crazy he'd been, would turn around and come back to me. And in that instant, I understood he'd left abruptly because he was afraid too. Afraid differently than me. He was afraid I'd say no and break his heart, so he ran before I could. And I'd been afraid—afraid that I'd say yes and end up breaking us both.

I had a poor track record when it came to marriage. Will deserved so much better than me. Maybe neither of us was ready. And maybe that was also evidenced in his rushed timing, my poor reaction, and his hasty departure.

It was ironic. I'd gotten past that fear in the dream—and believed that meant I'd also overcome my personal fears. But when it had counted, I'd been terrified.

And excited.

I was an emotional mess. I came inside and stood at the parlor window and watched for a very long time, but

Will didn't return, and finally I went to clear the dining room table and dispose of the untouched meal.

~~~~

He didn't come back. He didn't call. Nor did I.

As I washed up the dishes, I was angry. Angry at Will for proposing too soon. Angry at myself for handling it badly. As I walked through Wildflower House, turning off some lights and dimming others, I paused in the foyer. My eyes were caught by the photograph of the women and girls.

Everything here reminded me of someone, of people in my life now and in the past.

The framed photograph hanging above the foyer table was of the young women and teachers who'd lived here when the house was originally built and this had been a boarding and day school. Seth had seen the photo stored among the boxes and stuff at Sue's house, recognized it, and had given it to me. We'd almost become a couple, but then, by mutual agreement, we'd split. Seth was now in LA working a demanding, fast-paced marketing job in a big city. He was happy there. I was happy here.

My needlework here with all the rest seemed to bind me to them all, past and present, and to this place. Even the piano . . .

Will had played this piano.

I ran my fingers over the keys, and in the dim light as the echo of the last notes died away, and surrounded by memories and history, I crossed my arms, resting my
~~~~

hands on my shoulders.

Wildflower House had never felt so empty.

He'd said he wanted me to think about his proposal, and I'd said I would.

But that wasn't what he'd *hoped* for.

And then I was angry at myself again for acting as though Will and I were over.

I stood, pulling the key cover forward to close it.

We weren't over. Even if I said *not yet*, he'd stay.

But would it be the same between us?

I was angry again at Will for proposing too soon. At myself for not handling it better. If unwarranted worry was wasteful, then how much more pointless was this loop of anger and fear?

So I went to bed but couldn't rest. After tossing and turning for a while, I got up and wandered the house until I was standing on the back porch with a blanket wrapped around me.

I'd done the same after losing my father. I'd stood here on this back porch many times last summer, watching the night. Down the stairs to my right was the terrace with the outdoor furniture Dad had bought for me as a surprise soon after we'd moved in. The furniture was covered in fitted tarps now for the winter, and the cushions were stored inside the house, away from rodents who might be seeking a warm, cozy burrow. Directly in front of me lay the medallion garden with the sculpture in the center, all lit by the gentle, cool touch of the moon and stars above. And beneath the moonlit sky and the earthbound sculpture, my father's ashes rested in the polished urn I'd chosen. We'd buried him there—the three of us together—me, Will, and Nicole—in the medallion garden that Will had envisioned, then created with his own hands. And beyond the garden was the green slope of yard and the glittering reflections in the water of Cub Creek as it flowed by.

The grass was a less vibrant green than it would be come spring. The medallion garden area would bloom, first with the azaleas and later the rhododendrons. The wildflowers, less wild and widespread than when I'd first seen them, would also bloom. The tall pines bordering either side of the property would be the same regardless of the season, but the deciduous trees would be putting out buds and fresh green leaves. Earth would be stirring, restless in its own way.

As I was restless.

I didn't want to lose Will. Sometimes the difference between us seemed more than two years. Will would be taking on someone with history, and I would be taking on, in Will, someone who was less jaded and more centered.

He thought he knew what he wanted. Maybe I should trust him?

Victoria had accused me of wanting to control things. She was right. Whether that was my nature or a result of my childhood . . . most likely it was a double whammy of both.

I returned to bed, but that night sleep was hard to find.

Chapter Five

The day after Valentine's Day ~

The next morning, I rose soon after dawn. If I didn't hear from Will soon, I'd call him. If I knew what to say, I would already have called him.

I'd awakened with the certainty that we could reach a compromise. Was a wedding required, really? Perhaps we could work out something less official but still committed? Perhaps a long engagement? Something that would be easier to walk away from if either of us discovered that we had indeed made a big mistake?

I shrunk from that option because it felt less than honest. If I said yes to Will, it should be *yes*, not *probably*.

Laura had said she'd come over about midday, so this morning I was here alone with too much time to think.

Leaving the house, I followed the path around the side to where it joined the walkway between the old stone carriage house and the garden. Will had lit the walkway and the garden and the carriage house at Christmas, and he'd left the lights up, though we didn't turn them on most evenings. But we could when we began holding events.

We. Who was *we*?

Victoria had asked that question. Victoria had a sharper intellect than many gave her credit for.

I pushed aside the door to the carriage house and stood in the doorway, remembering how Will had wired the room for music the night of the Christmas open house and how we'd danced to "Christmas Waltz."

Be still, my heart.

Light filtered in through the high window, turning the dust motes and bits of flyaway hay into sparkles. Magical. And that was fitting. The evening of the Christmas open house had been absolutely magical—in large part *because* of Will.

Closing the door behind me, I moved inside, mesmerized. I reached up to grasp at the dust motes. There were countless bits of light and glitter dancing in the rays of sunshine streaming in from a window high above. I captured them, holding them carefully, tightly between my hands. But when I opened my hands, there was nothing to be seen. Only air. Because human hands can't catch light, much less hold on to it.

This main room was mostly empty now except for a plain wooden bench along one wall. In one corner a set of narrow stairs led up to a small room. I sat on the bench, feeling listless, and pulled at a loose bit of yarn in my sweater. More light flooded in as the door opened.

Will said, "Hi, Kara."

I glanced up at him. His expression reflected what I, myself, was feeling.

"How did you guess I was in here?"

"You weren't in the house. The doors are unlocked, in case you didn't know."

"Isn't that how we do things out in the country?" I asked with a wry smile. "I'm expecting Aunt Laura later."

He nodded. "Mind if I join you?"

"I wish you would."

"Have you thought about the question I asked?"

"I've thought of little else."

"Figured as much." He paused. "First off, let me say I'm sorry."

"Sorry?"

"For being so clumsy about it. You'd never guess that I'd practiced. And the nerves still got me." After a pause, he continued, "And you don't have an answer yet, I can see, but I thought you might like someone to chew all those thoughts over with."

"You?"

He shrugged with a smile. "Who better? This concerns you and me." He sat beside me on the bench, thigh touching thigh.

"True," I said. I reached over and took his hand. "You and I have been seeing each other almost daily for months now, though only in recent months as more than just . . . well, as people with feelings for each other. But what do we really know?" I squeezed his hand. "Not suggesting you're hiding anything, but we each have personal histories that we really haven't discussed."

"Like about your mother taking off when you were a kid? Growing up with your dad, who was successful in business but had his own limitations? I know things didn't go well with your first marriage. I've had some heartbreaks and general mistakes myself." He shrugged. "None of that predicts anything about how you and I will go forward together."

Listening to him, I could almost believe that my scars, visible and not, didn't matter.

I persisted, "What about the basics? We haven't talked about what we want for our future. Where we'll live, our hopes, dreams . . . and even about children."

"All important things," he agreed.

"Definitely."

"We'll find out together." He paused, then asked, "What would you like in terms of a wedding?"

I shivered.

"That bad?"

"No, Will. I'm sorry. I'm having trouble getting past my history. I don't want to hurt you. I worry about that."

"I'm tougher than you think. So, the question stands. Not an answer to the *big* question, but just in the abstract. For the ceremony . . . big or small?"

Could I play along? I tried, for his sake.

"There are so many people in our lives. Once we start inviting one or two, then twenty more will spring to mind. I never would've thought I'd know so many people—people that I'd consider inviting to my . . . a wedding."

"True. So, we'd keep it private. Elope."

"But then they'll be hurt. All those well-wishers. Your mother and sister . . . you're her only son."

"True."

I added my other hand to the one already clutching his

hand.

"Will, please forgive me for suggesting this after your proposal, but do we have to go through the formalities? Couldn't we just go on as we are? Aren't we good together already?"

"It's not enough, Kara. Not for us. You know that."

"But we can continue to grow our relationship . . . I want that too. We'll just put off the *official* stuff for now. We have options, Will."

He gave me a sad smile. "Tempting idea, but no. I'm too greedy, Kara. I want it all, for better or for worse. I want it official. I want everyone to know that we have committed our lives to each other."

I squeezed his hand. "But Wildflower House, Will. The creative retreat. Where would we live? If I'm going to have overnight guests, how would that work? Your apartment is too far away . . ."

"And too small. But we aren't limited. As you said, we have options." He stood. "I guess you need to figure out which direction you're going in with Wildflower House." He grimaced. "I don't really see you operating a bed-and-breakfast. Playing host to couples looking for quaint and cozy, year after year? No. Hiring someone to play hostess for you? I don't see that working either. Probably not right for this location anyway. Anything else—the creative retreat and event place for weddings and such—will be mostly day events."

He shrugged. "Do you need to live elsewhere? Whether I'm with you or not, I mean."

He walked toward the door, but stopped there.

"Regardless of what you do with Wildflower House, we can make the living arrangements work with it or around it." He looked down at his shoes, then back at me. "For the record, I've never been married. Never even been engaged. No children that I know of. Never did jail time." He offered a tiny grin. "That's an important point, right?" He shrugged. "I meant what I said about giving you time to think. But not too long, okay? Don't get lost in the details, Kara. If you need a long engagement, we can do that. The heart of the matter is . . . well, what matters. And if in all that thinking, you discover that I'm wrong about your feelings, then tell me that too. Don't keep me hanging on, please, if you decide you don't love me."

He left.

Stupid, I called myself. *A thousand times stupid,* as Victoria might say. Why couldn't I just say the *YES* word? I should chase after him, tackle him, saying, "A thousand times yes." There was a part of me that wanted nothing more than to do exactly that.

I trusted Will. It was myself I didn't trust.

I stayed in the carriage house for a while, sitting and thinking . . . about details.

Details. They were as elusive and fickle as words, changing with each possibility or shift in the wind. In the end, the details must matter in some way, to some degree, but they were truly nothing more than extras and were definitely *not* the heart of the matter.

Will was right about that.

Back when I was having trouble committing to turning Wildflower House into the retreat and event space

I envisioned, Nicole had pointed out to me that I'd never learned to act of my own volition. As a child, I'd done whatever seemed necessary to keep my mother from leaving, I'd learned to function—quite well, actually—in tandem with my father, but I'd had to interact with him within his narrow emotional bandwidth. Even with Niles, I'd accommodated his preferences.

I wasn't willing to fall back into that same pattern with Will. I would blame us both later.

But what did I want? I shook my head and sighed. The dust motes danced on, but I was too tired and discouraged to join in.

~~~~

When I returned to the house, Laura said, "Will just left. Did he find you? Is he okay?"

She was seated in the workroom in front of the computer. I stood in the doorway. "He did. Why do you ask?"

"He didn't seem quite himself."

I forced a quick smile. "He's fine. Just distracted by something else."

She gave me a long look. "What about you? You seem distracted too."

I didn't acknowledge her question, but instead asked, "Ready to get back to entering the receipts in the worksheet?"

"If that's what will be helpful. I want to be useful to you."
~~~~

"Oh." Her face said it all, and it was suddenly clear to me. "You don't enjoy this kind of work, do you? I thought you were just struggling to get the hang of it."

"No, really, it's okay. I'm getting better at it all the time."

I walked across the room and sat in the chair beside hers. "No." I shook my head. "I was happy to pass this task on to you because I dislike data entry so much, but you don't enjoy it either, and I'm sorry I was so slow to understand."

"What didn't you understand?" Nicole walked in. Without pausing for an answer, she said, "Maddie went straight back to the kitchen." Nicole focused on me. "Said she knew where the cookies were?"

"She does indeed." I marveled that I was even surprised that Nicole had let herself in. Open-door policy prevailed here at Wildflower House . . . even when I tried to keep the doors locked.

"I have a showing this afternoon, and Mom has a doctor's appointment."

"Does Mel need a ride?"

"No, indeed. As you know, she's back to driving, but with the added distraction of the doctor's visit, she gets nervous about it since the stent went in, so she's having a friend drive her." Nicole shared a brief and rare smile. "She feels more independent going with a friend instead of with her eagle-eyed, worrisome daughter."

I nodded. "Sounds like Mel. Glad she's doing well enough to have the option of choosing how to get there."

"Yes, true. Anyway, I'll be back in plenty of time to

pick Maddie up for supper. Any problem?"

"No, she's always welcome."

Laura added her voice to mine. "She's so sweet."

"So then, what's the misunderstanding between you two? Did I hear you say data entry?"

It took me a moment to realize she was referring back to when she'd first walked into the room—to what she'd heard me saying to Laura, not to the . . . issue between Will and me.

"Yes, but it's not something Laura enjoys."

"Then hire someone who does."

"Easily said."

She ignored me. "There are other things that need attention that I suspect Laura could be helpful with. For instance, you need a website. You need promotional materials. You have artisans lined up for the pottery classes, painting, and such as that, but you need brochures and pamphlets with scheduling and pricing to offer potential students and clients, not to mention being sure you have the right, actual stuff needed for the classes. If you've already got those tasks down, tell me, but I'm guessing not."

She crossed her arms and kept her gaze pinned on me. "You are a big-picture thinker, not someone who nails down details. Laura has a way with people. She has such a pleasant manner and is patient. Have her research what you're missing, what should go on the website. Maybe call around to some other facilities in the region and pick their brains."

Nicole finished with a look at me that I understood.

She was communicating that she knew those were tasks I'd hate even more than data entry. Meanwhile, Laura's face had brightened. She looked eager.

"I can get information for you, Kara, make notes and suggestions to complement the info you've already assembled, and then you can make the decisions."

"I started work on those things, including the website, but never pulled it all together." I looked at Laura. "If you're game to try, I'll pass the folder on to you and give you a chance to flesh it out."

She nodded.

I waved at the laptop and the table and the piles of papers, saying to her, "Walk away from that spreadsheet stuff. I'll work on it when I'm watching TV or such."

Nicole said, "What's with Will? He walked past me outside, looking like a thundercloud."

Trust Nicole to ask the question that I didn't want voiced. Before I could speak, Laura said, "I thought so too."

Nicole gave me another close look. "Did you and he have a disagreement? Which reminds me . . . when you two get married, are you planning to—"

"Enough." I held up a hand to shut down this topic. "Stop. We aren't getting married."

"Not today, maybe." Nicole frowned. "But anyone can see—"

"No, Nicole."

"I was just going to say that you shouldn't allow other considerations like Maddie Lyn or Mel or such to interfere with plans, and I was wondering . . ." She stopped.

Laura asked, "Are you and Will discussing . . ."

I glared at her. Her posture slumped a little, and she trailed off.

Nicole said, "Kara. I'm sorry if I've touched on a sore point." She shook her head. "I didn't mean to interfere, but people talk, as you know." She sighed. "Don't be touchy about it, whether it's true or not. If you don't want to discuss it or encourage them to discuss it with others, then laugh it off. Just laugh it off. Practice doing that." She paused. "They don't mean harm. It's just that anyone who sees the two of you together—they know. Even if you don't know it yet yourself."

Nicole left us. I'd offended her. Heaven knew, maybe she'd earned a rebuff . . . but not really.

Following her out to the porch, I said, "Nicole."

She turned to me. "Yes?"

I stepped down, away from the house, lowering my voice. I had to ask. "Did Will speak to you about anything . . . about him and me?"

With a tiny shake of her head, she said, "No." She pressed her lips together in a way that I found revealing, and I was suspicious, but then she added, looking away, "When I see the two of you together, I remember how it was with Henry and me. We let so much time go by . . . and then he was gone unexpectedly. I wonder sometimes . . ."

"Was it my fault, Nicole? Did I interfere with the plans you and Dad had made when I moved here with him?"

She shook her head with a sad smile. "No. Maybe."

She shrugged. "But we had seven years during which we could've made that kind of commitment to each other, and we didn't. Maybe we aren't . . . weren't . . . the kind of people built for that. For commitment. For sure, we didn't try hard enough, and now we'll never know."

There was a forlorn note to her voice, almost as if she'd forgotten I was there.

I said softly, "Thanks for the advice about how to manage remarks. I'll practice nonchalance while looking in the mirror, as you suggested. I suppose Will and I do give folks ideas."

She shrugged. "Folks get ideas regardless. I think it's more about them wishing you well than meaning to interfere. The two of you mesh . . . in some odd way that I won't try to explain. I think you already feel that . . . the inevitability, maybe? At any rate, I hope the advice helps." She started moving again toward the car, then stopped, resting her hand on the hood. When she looked up, she shielded her eyes, probably against the sun, though I caught the glint of light on her cheek, perhaps the sun catching a small tear.

"Watch the time, Kara. I wish Henry and I had done a better job of that, instead of just assuming . . ." She cleared her throat and gave her whole body a shake. "See you later."

She drove away.

I stood there for a long minute, staring after her. She and my dad had met when she was his real estate agent for a long-ago house purchase when he lived in Richmond. They'd had a relationship that spanned years and that I hadn't even been aware of until we'd moved here and I'd seen them interacting. Was that what she'd meant by people seeing me and Will together? Of course. And while Will and I believed we were well behaved and discreet, we also clearly enjoyed being together. We always seemed to be entangled in each other's arms.

We'd only been fooling ourselves.

Finally, I turned and went back into the house to find Maddie. By now, she'd probably emptied the cookie tin.

But no. Laura was with her. Maddie had arranged her small dishes on the kitchen table, and Laura had poured a tiny bit of tea in each little cup.

The two of them were sipping their tea and discussing a movie Maddie had seen—some version of *The Nutcracker*—and the young character, Clara. Maddie Lyn was saying she knew how to dance too, and did Aunt Laura want to see?

Quietly, I left them there. My heart ached. I returned to the carriage house to cry privately and in peace.

CHAPTER SIX

Two days after Valentine's Day ~

That night, the dream returned.

This time, the dream had less the feel of a warning, but was more bittersweet. In this iteration, when Will vanished from sight, I woke, as before, but with tears on my cheeks and thinking of Nicole and my father. Of so many missed opportunities of so many kinds. Of regret.

It was only the second day post-proposal, but this had gone on long enough. I couldn't stand it, and I was certain Will felt the same.

When daylight arrived, and as early as it seemed reasonable, I called Will and left him a voice mail asking him to come by. I hadn't seen him since we'd talked in the carriage house yesterday. It felt like an age.

When he showed up, when I could see him face-to-face, I'd insist that we discuss at least a few details, and then we'd reach a rational decision together—surely a yes—I wanted it to be yes—and then we could move forward with both of us knowing exactly what we were signing up for. He did leave a voice mail. For whatever reason, my phone didn't ring. I saw the notification flash on the phone screen. His message said, "I'll come by about lunchtime."

And that was it.

Okay. Fair enough, I told myself. *Now get back to work.*

I joined Laura in the workroom. She was messing around with text and images for brochures.

"Wow," I said. "You've really jumped right in, haven't you?"

Her face was bright as she looked at me. "Yes, I'm enjoying this very much. I'll try not to let you down."

I shook my head. "You won't. You're going to do this brilliantly. Let me know if you need info or whatever from me."

"Will do." And she went right back to work with the images and text while I sat at the computer fiddling with the business plan and the expense spreadsheet.

Of course, I kept thinking of Will.

I was more annoyed than worried. He'd left a voice mail, after all. Even so, I sent a text, just in case he'd missed the ones I'd already sent.

I smiled at the foolishness of my ego. Will might've lost his phone, or perhaps he'd left it in the truck while he was working.

Or maybe he'd changed his mind. Maybe he was regretting his proposal? I was very controlling. It was true. I found myself rising from the seat, but I sat again, breathing deeply.

No, no, and no. I told myself not to be so needy. Such

a diva. Practically neurotic. Someone who expected others to put them above all else? No, that wasn't me. Of course not. I wasn't that person. It was just nerves and that ridiculous feeling that something was wrong. Very wrong.

Suddenly chilled, as if a huge draft had swept through the room, I shivered.

"Kara, are you okay?"

"Me?" I looked up, realizing I'd been staring at the computer screen and accomplishing nothing. "I'm fine. Just fine."

"Go take a walk or something, please."

"What?"

She was holding a pair of scissors. A bottle of glue, unopened, was near at hand. She was still playing with the arrangements of images and text blocks on paper. No computer program. But she was so engaged with the creation that I suspected she might transition to online graphic design tools with much less trouble than she'd had with that daggone spreadsheet.

"This looks good, Aunt Laura. Very good, in fact. I like this image with the potter's wheels. And the stargazing one too. I wonder if we want to highlight both indoor and outdoor activities?"

"Kara, if you want to talk, I'm happy to listen, but for this, please let me work on it for a while before we discuss it." She looked stern. "For now, you're driving me a little crazy with your fidgeting. I'll finish laying out the images and text blocks. Go get some air and exercise, and I'll find you when the ad is ready for review."

Ouch. But she was right. I left her there and went to

the kitchen.

Grabbing my coat and putting on my low boots with the furry insides, I walked out the back door and down to the bridge over Cub Creek. It was a small bridge, and the air was chilly, but the water made a pretty sound, very musical. I could've kept going and even visited Mel, but I was calmer now. My perspective had readjusted itself, and I could almost laugh at my foolishness . . . but not quite. Something wasn't right.

I returned to the house. Laura found me in the kitchen as I was hanging my coat on the hook and ditching the boots.

She said, "I'm sorry I was short with you. Is there anything I can do?"

Slightly embarrassed, I smiled. "I'm the one who's sorry. I wanted to speak with Will, but he isn't returning my texts, and he didn't show up at lunchtime as he'd said he would. Shame on me for letting it bug me."

"Oh," Laura said. "Well, Will called earlier this morning as I was leaving home. He'd offered to check on something for me, a part for my furnace." She shrugged. "He said he'd see me over here about lunchtime. I did wonder if you might be fidgety because he was coming . . . or because he didn't." Suddenly, her eyes widened. "And I never told you I'd spoken to him. I'm so sorry. Should I have?"

"I'm sure he's okay. He probably got held up somewhere." But I wasn't sure at all.

"That's possible. He said he was stopping by the Lange property before coming to Wildflower."

Now I was truly a mess inside. I tried to hide it, but the Lange property . . . the dream . . . everything was putting me on edge. I was tired of it. Why must it be so hard just to spend a little time being happy?

"I'm sorry I didn't tell you."

Aunt Laura was doing the hand thing that would soon go from clasped hands to wringing digits.

I assured her, "No problem. He was probably interrupted or got delayed. No more than that. And please, I don't want you to ever feel caught in the middle."

"You look worried."

"No—or mostly no. I feel uneasy about clearing the property."

"You don't want to?"

"No, I do. That's what's so crazy."

"Well, you'll figure it out. I'm always impressed by your courage and determination." She gave me a hug. "I'll bet that's exactly how my brother, Henry, was. I missed seeing him in action, but I'm blessed to be able to be part of your life." She left the kitchen.

I let her go. Had Will been held up somewhere? Maybe he was stuck where he didn't have reliable cell service? I picked up my phone, thinking I'd try one more time. Will hadn't come to Wildflower at lunchtime, I knew that much, but he might have gone to the Lange property. He could've driven out along Route 522, parked on the side of the road, and cut through the woods to get there on foot. By the end of that thought, I'd slid my boots back on and my feet had taken me to the front door. My coat was somehow over my arm, and I pulled it on.

There were no vehicles parked out front except mine and Laura's.

I stepped out onto the porch so I could see the larger parking area.

There it was. My heart warmed. Will's truck was parked away from the house, in the lot. But unless he'd managed to squeeze down onto the floorboard or was stretched out in the truck bed, he wasn't in it.

"Did you leave your phone in the truck, Will?" Had I spoken aloud? Yes, I thought I had. And by then I was hurrying along the short path to the parking lot.

Yes, the truck was empty. Standing beside the driver's door, I dialed his number. It rang on my phone, but there was no answering ring coming from inside Will's truck. I tried the door handle. Unlocked. I searched the seat and the console. No sign of his phone.

And still no answer.

I ran into the house. "Laura?"

Laura was already at the office door. "Is something wrong?"

"I don't think so, but Will—"

"I knew it. I just knew it. What can I do?"

I put my hands on Laura's arms. "Calm down. It's all good. Will's truck is parked in the lot, so if he was going out to the Lange property then he must've walked via the creek path. He isn't answering his phone—maybe it lost its charge or something. I'm going to take a walk out there myself, just in case."

"I'll come with you."

"Thank you, but it's best if you wait here in case he

shows up. You can tell him where I went."

She nodded. "Okay, sure. Okay."

I tried not to look anxious. I tried to move easily away and walk as casually as I could, but my unease was growing. It was nearly overwhelming.

But why? I asked myself. Will had been out to that lot any number of times, as had I. And I shivered again, unable to warm up despite my coat.

With my phone in hand, I hurried down the back steps and across the back lawn, past the medallion garden. Ignoring the nooks in the woods, I headed straight toward the creek near where the path to the Lange property began. When I reached the path, I hurried along, watching for roots and rocks. It wouldn't do to stumble or fall.

I remembered having felt there was something wrong with that place back when I'd first gone there with my father. That memory assailed me again, and I moved all the faster. I knew, without doubt and reason, that I'd find Will there. If I did, and if he was okay, I was going to give him a piece of my mind, whether he deserved it or not.

Cub Creek flowed through Louisa County. It started somewhere north of the Wildflower House property and continued mostly southward, bisecting the county, and it kept going until the waters reached the South Anna River. From Wildflower to the old Lange property, Will and his crew had improved the path for me with the idea that it would be a lovely, easy wooded walk for the guests I planned to host in the future. I was walking that path now, and the only sounds around me were those of the moving water and the birds.

This time of year, the woods were quiet, resting up for spring, but today the birds were busy, and they were doing a lot of chirping and singing back and forth. I heard them, but only on the edge of my consciousness, because I was thinking of Will. Of his smile, sometimes shy, sometimes brash. His dark hair and perilous blue eyes. His understated manner that sometimes masqueraded as shyness but was in truth the cool surface demeanor of a deep-thinking, passionate man. A man good with plants, with building things, able to understand design and implementation.

And why was I thinking of him as if this was some sort of eulogy? Because I'd lost my father less than a year ago? And my husband before that? Maybe that feeling of bad luck and loss was still lingering below the surface, ready to pop out as soon as something seemed iffy?

Finally, I reached the big rocks. The path ended just beyond them, and a lesser path turned inland, disappearing almost entirely as it entered a group of sticker bushes. I was mindful of the stickers as I pushed aside the spindly branches, and soon the caved-in roof of the house was visible ahead. Vines ran rampant across the building and along the ground, covering much of the trash—the shards of glass, rusted metal, and nails that could cut flesh so easily and brutally.

There was no sound. No Will. Nothing that indicated he was here.

Had I overreacted? Had he left his truck back at the house and gotten a ride with one of his workers somewhere else? That was possible. I could call his boss,

Jim Mitchell, and ask where Will was working today, but I didn't have Jim's number. Will might not thank me for doing that, anyway. Clearly, I was making something out of nothing.

I stood there trying to recall exactly where the well was and other possible hazards less visible because of the layers of wet, matted leaves and fallen branches. I didn't want to trip in a hole and end up with a sprained ankle, maybe a broken leg, out here by myself.

So cold, I shivered again, telling myself that Will wasn't here and that I should go home. This had been a silly, panicked, wasted effort. I should call Laura and let her know it was a false alarm. Instead, I stepped forward for a closer look and saw his cap—his bright orange billed cap with the Mitchell's logo on it.

I left it there on the ground, almost superstitious about moving it, as if doing so might break a crucial link to Will.

Where was he?

I held my breath, and in that silent moment I heard a noise. Maybe a creak.

"Will?" I whispered. Then I dragged in a deep breath and yelled, "Will? Are you here, Will?"

"Hey. Kara."

His voice sounded low. Muffled. I scanned the clearing, the debris, the trees.

"Will! Where are you?"

"Watch out, Kara. Watch your step."

His voice seemed to be coming from the other side of the house, from what must've been the backyard, which was littered with rubble and rotten boards and twisted, rusted metal.

"Will?" I was almost in tears at this point as I hastily picked my way there. I blinked to clear my vision. A low screeching noise came from nearby.

"I'm in here, Kara." His voice came from somewhere within the debris and sounded almost disembodied. "Under some boards. Some concrete, I think. Maybe a cellar. It caved in. Stay away."

I started to rush forward. "I'll get you out of there."

"No. Stop. Get help."

"Yes, I'll call 911."

"Call Jim. If you can't get him, then call 911."

"But—"

"Tell Jim I fell into some sort of cavity. Like a cellar. I don't think I'm injured."

All I could see before me was a large, broken section of shingled roof that had fallen and lay slanted across the top of general debris. It was far too large and heavy for me to attempt to move it.

"Will, please. I don't have his number."

"My cap. Do you see it? Under the cap."

I hurried back to retrieve his cap and found his phone beneath. I knew his code—his birthday—and unlocked it.

Will hadn't spoken again. The silence unnerved me. I searched his contacts and found Jack's number, but my cold, clumsy fingers had trouble doing their part. Finally, it was ringing, and I was already picking my way back through debris to where I'd last heard Will's voice. The call connected as I sank to the ground next to a sliver of dark space between the edge of the roof and the ground. I presumed the hole continued under the debris that blocked me from seeing more. The damp, dark earth soaked through the knees of my jeans instantly.

"Mitchell's Lawn and Landscaping. Jim here."

"Jim . . . It's Will . . ."

"Kara? Is that you? Will's not here. Are you okay?"

"No. Yes." Breathless, I was now lying on my stomach near the edge of the hole, peering into the darkness. I said, "Will needs help. I wanted to call 911, but he insisted I call you."

"Take a breath, then tell me."

Calm. Stay calm.

"We're out at the Lange property. Near the old house. Will has fallen into some sort of hole, a cavity, but there's lots of debris on top. He said it's like an old cellar." I repeated, "I wanted to call 911."

"Is he hurt?"

Sounds of movement were interwoven with Jim's voice. He was already in motion.

"He says he isn't, but he doesn't sound right. He said to call you. That you'd know what to do."

Like a knife, the memory hit me of kneeling beside my father in the field of flowers, waiting for a rescue squad as he died. Not their fault. He was gone too quickly for anyone to save him. But Will wasn't. He was here, though silent.

Jim said, "I'll call 911 and get them out there immediately, and I'll coordinate with the sheriff's department. You're with Will?"

"I am. I'm beside the hole—whatever it is."

"Be very careful, Kara. Understand? Don't get yourself hurt too, and if Will says he's okay, then leave him as he is. We'll get him out of there."

"You know the way?" My voice sounded small. Running down.

"I do. Hang in there, Kara. He'll be okay."

Jim disconnected. To get on the road. To make calls to the right people.

I thanked God that Jim Mitchell knew the right people. That's why Will had insisted I call him. And I prayed Jim truly would know what to do.

"Will? Did you hear all that?" I waited, then asked again, "Will?"

"Yes. He's coming?"

His voice sounded a bit labored.

"Yes. He is."

"It'll all be fine, Kara."

His voice sounded weak. He'd said he wasn't hurt. Maybe he was *too* hurt to realize it. Or hadn't wanted to frighten me.

I fought fear and tears. I reached down into the darkness, into that crevice formed by the shingles and rotting wood, and there was a smell that made my stomach turn over. But my fingers couldn't touch Will, or even sense his warmth. I rested my hand on the roof and put my head, now so heavy, down on my bent arm that was against the ground. That frigid ground. The dampness crept into my bones. How much worse must it be for Will?

"Can I help you in any way?" I asked.

"You are."

He'd answered. The relief almost overwhelmed me.

"What can I do, Will?"

"You already did it." After a pause, he added, "I'm sorry this happened. I'm glad you found me."

"Me too."

"Not sure how I would've dug myself out of this on my own." He coughed. "But I would've. I promise you that I would've found my way out and back to you."

"Oh, Will." It took me a moment to get control again. "Jim said to wait here. Should I go up to the road? Flag down folks?"

"No. Jim knows. Just wait. Here."

We both fell silent. The sound of his voice . . . It seemed like speaking might be weakening him.

"You don't have to say anything. You sound uncomfortable. It's okay." I added, "I'm sure they'll be here soon."

"Talk to me, Kara."

About what? My brain suddenly seemed empty. I thought of Laura telling me he'd called.

"Laura told me you'd called, but not right away. She was doing mock-ups of promotional material." What else could I say? I added, "I'm actually amazed by her. She's found a niche, for sure. But I'd been going a little crazy, wondering *why* you hadn't called me back and didn't come at lunchtime either. And all the time you were here. Laura felt so badly about not telling me you'd called and were coming out here first. When she finds out you were in danger, she's going to feel even worse."

When he didn't respond, I couldn't help myself. I

said, “Will?”

No answer.

“Will,” I repeated. “If the offer is still open, I accept.”

I heard a shifting noise and a groan, followed by his voice. “I knew you would . . . if . . . you thought about . . . it.”

“You were right.” I added sternly, “Don’t disappoint me, Will. My heart can’t bear it.”

“I promise.”

In the distance, I heard noises and a man’s voice raised in a shout. I listened, pretty sure I also heard the distant sound of heavy equipment forcing its way through the overgrown and rutted dirt road, driving this way.

“Someone’s coming, Will.”

“’Kay.”

I rose to my feet. My jeans and my coat were dirty, soaked with dark earth. My hands were pale and shaking. I shivered again, suddenly cold all the way through.

It wasn’t Jim Mitchell who strode out of the woods. It was a tall, dark-haired man dressed in a uniform. As he came closer, I saw he was a county deputy.

“Kara Hart?”

“Yes, that’s me. I’m fine. It’s Will Mercer who’s in trouble.” I pointed at the roof and boards. “Will is down in there.” And he was too quiet. I cried out, “Will? Will?”

The officer touched my arm lightly. “I’m Dan Wheeler, Kara. Deputy. Do you mind if I call you Kara?”

Forced by the habit of courtesy and civility, I looked at him. His expression was serious, but his dark eyes were kind.

"Of course, but we have to get Will out of there." Hearing the growing panic in my voice, I stopped and breathed slowly.

"We will." He turned toward the debris pile. "Will? Can you hear me?"

"Dan?"

My knees went weak, and I felt the deputy's hand on my arm.

"Good," he said, speaking to Will, his voice cool and calm. "Hold on, Will. Jim and the others are on their way. How are you doing?"

"Fine. I'm okay. Just stuck. Don't want to shift what's on top of me without some help from above." There was an odd sort of gasping laugh, and he added, "Well, I can always use help from *Above*, but for now you and Jim will have to do."

Dan laughed with him. It made me angry.

"Not a time for joking. This is not a game."

"Kara," Will said, but Dan cut him off.

He said, "I'm going to move Kara back to a safer distance."

I tried to shake his hand from my arm. "No, I'm staying here."

His tone was unyielding, though his voice was gentle and even. "You can stand nearby, but not here. You will be in the way here. I know you don't want that. We all want to get Will out safely."

Before the soft, sodden old earth gives way and caves in the rest of the way, bringing more concrete and metal down on top of him. Somehow, I heard the words in my head. Like a whispered, urgent message. Those images felt even more real than the ones I'd experienced during the January snowstorm when I'd imagined Will running off an icy road—an empty fear that hadn't happened. This one was different. It was playing out before me. But I fixed my mind on the belief that this wouldn't go wrong either. I visualized Will rescued, well and safe.

I nodded. "I understand."

"Let's go this way. Watch your step because we can't know how large the cavity is."

"I'll be nearby, Will."

No answer.

The deputy nudged me into motion. I watched my footing. I was ever so careful because I wouldn't risk delaying Will's rescue by so much as a heartbeat.

He guided me around to the far side, away from the house debris and toward the more open area where the path met the clearing. He asked, "Are you all right?"

"I'm fine. Just get Will out."

"We will." He pointed to the path. "The others are bringing equipment through that way, so stay over here."

"I will, Deputy."

He nodded and gave an encouraging smile. "*Dan* will work."

Before he moved away, I stopped him with my hand on his arm. "You know Will. You're his friend?"

"I am."

"Okay, then. Go get him out of there and bring him back to me."

"Yes, ma'am."

He hadn't gone far when the noises I'd been hearing grew closer. Distantly, I noted the sound of my phone ringing, but I ignored it. My attention—my absolute focus—was needed here, on rescuing Will. Jim entered the clearing. He cast a glance toward the deputy, who walked toward him and pointed to the area where Will was imprisoned.

Imprisoned. Was he breathing in there? What if they moved the wrong thing and something shifted or collapsed in a terrible way? Loss assailed me. The cold, deadly feel of it pierced me. I'd lost people before. Too many. I couldn't bear it again. Suddenly, a sharp, icy shiver racked me. And then a warm hand touched me.

"Libbie?" I was surprised.

"I came with Jim. I hope you don't mind. I know we've only met once."

I struggled to breathe properly. I must've been holding my breath. By being here, she was pulling my attention away from Will's dark place. A rush of resentment startled me.

She said, "We both care about Will."

"We do."

I grabbed her hand. "He's gotten so quiet. His voice . . . and then he hardly spoke at all. Now, there's . . ."

Libbie's face went blank for a split second, then she said, "Well, he's in a really awkward place." She squeezed my hand. "Did you know that I was in an auto accident a while back? It was very serious. But Jim and Dan make an effective team. They know exactly who to call on for help.

They'll get Will out of there."

I was suddenly angry. So angry. "What was he doing messing around out here anyway?" I gasped. "Oh, wait, that's not fair. He and I discussed clearing this property. But he should've waited and not come out here alone. I wanted him to stay away from this place. Suppose I hadn't found him?"

"But you did. You found him. He goes lots of places, and some of them are tricky or potentially dangerous. He's smart and works safely, but sometimes stuff happens—like with my accident—and if we're lucky, the people who love us are able to rescue us."

"But—"

"But, as someone once explained to me, you can't make them afraid or secretive because you fear for them, or fear losing them. That's not fair to them. Some people are confident risk-takers. Not foolish or overconfident, but simply confident. And that's important." She was holding my hand in both of hers by now. "That's who they are and part of why we love them."

I looked toward the woods and the sound machinery.

Libbie spoke softly. "Jim said they couldn't get the bigger equipment back here without improving the dirt road, but we had a smaller excavator with a grapple parked at the Cub Creek location and he was able to get it up on the trailer in a jiffy. That's what you're hearing and it's almost here."

Yes, I saw it through the trees as it neared the clearing.

"Right behind the excavator is Winslow. He heard the call on the scanner and offered his help. He has this wrecker . . .”

“Wrecker?” I didn’t like the sound of that.

“It’s actually called a boom truck with a winch, and he takes it most everywhere. He’s very talented with it but his truck couldn’t make it through on its own. It’s following right behind the excavator.” She tightened her grip on my hand. “No, stay here. Don’t distract them. They don’t know exactly what’s wedged down there with Will and how it might shift. They’ll go slow and we’ll be patient, so everyone comes out of this safe and sound.”

I heard iron in her voice. And she was right. I waited.

After the vehicles were in place, ropes and chains were arranged around the roof part. I tried to watch the activity, as if a moment of my personal inattention could cause disaster—which was ridiculous, of course. Each time, Libbie moved slightly behind me and spoke softly again, sort of forcing me to turn toward her. Even as it occurred to me that there might be an ulterior motive to the maneuver, I allowed it. That knife in my gut—the pain eased from sharp to dull.

They raised that large section carefully, checking to be sure that it was holding together and watching for movement that might warn of other things shifting. Apparently, it was going well. As the roof was lifted and set aside, I sensed the decrease in tension in the physical actions of the rescuers and in the tone of their voices. Two men came out of the woods bearing a long ladder, and I saw another group in uniforms, both men and women, who I believed to be the emergency medical workers. They approached the core group around the cavity carefully, and people were pointing. The voices were calm and low, except for someone occasionally raising their voice to communicate something specifically.

I pulled away from Libbie. "Thank you. I'll stay clear, but I must be closer." These people had the power to help him that I didn't have, but Will was mine. Mine. And I had to see.

She nodded but kept her hand on my arm as we moved a fraction closer to the action.

Standing there as debris was lifted, hearing smaller debris fall farther into the abyss, wondering if worse would happen, seeing someone descend partway in to check on Will, the bits of exchanged conversation—it was the hope, the shared belief, and the evidence of the team effort that kept me from losing my mind. And when it looked like they were ready to lift Will out, Libbie's hands tightened on my arm like a vise.

"Almost there," she said. "Give them room to work and the thinking space to take care of Will."

Thinking space? My thinking space only had room for one long, jumbled thought. I'd missed too many opportunities in my life, many of which I'd had no control over—Mom leaving, Dad dying—even Niles and all that went with his choice to violate our marriage. But this time? *This time, I still had a chance.*

They brought him out secured in a litter. He was lifted over the edge, and other hands stretched out to receive him. He was tall and no lightweight, and I was afraid they'd drop him, but they managed, and other hands reached down to help the helpers out.

Will was an absolute mess, covered in black mud and so still that it was good that Libbie had held me back. I would've thrown myself onto him and the litter, sure that he was already gone. But then his arm moved, his hand lifting. His face turned toward one of the men steadying the litter.

Even as the litter that bore him settled on the gurney, the remaining debris where he'd been trapped shifted like it was having its own private earthquake. Something metal collided with something else. It didn't matter because Will was already out of there, but the vibration, the wave of noise, filled the air as if something was wailing because its prize had escaped it. And maybe the metallic, rending sound of it touched old memories from my own car crash. Regardless of why, I fainted.

Libbie still had her grip on my arm, and Dan was nearby, so luckily I didn't fall flat-out. I like to think that I sank rather gracefully to the ground and regained consciousness even as my knees hit earth and I felt a hand on my arm and someone else's arm around my back, supporting me, as one of my helpers lifted me and sat me down on a log. I sat there shaken but otherwise fine.

I told the people around me, "Take care of Will, please."

And then Will's voice was calling out, "What's wrong? Is she okay?"

A man said, "Stay put, Will. She's fine. Let me finish getting your vitals."

Will yelled, "Kara, what's wrong?"

The man working on him said, "You need stitches at

the very least and to get that wound on your head checked out. Those ribs are badly bruised. Maybe fractured."

I told Libbie, "I have to speak with him."

She didn't argue as I stood, but she kept a hold on my arm, and Dan hovered, apparently ready to catch me should I take another dive into unconsciousness.

"I'm fine now," I repeated, and walked over to Will.

He was still strapped to the gurney, which was parked, but his legs were moving as if he was planning an escape.

"Will," I said, moving close and touching his grimy face. "You smell awful. Which is my way of saying I don't know what you came into contact with down in that pit, but you need to get checked out and get stitches and some sort of antiseptic cleaning before you get an awful infection. Heaven knows what you may have breathed in."

"I've been hurt worse."

"Go. Let them take you to the hospital. I'll meet you there."

I saw the stubbornness in his blue eyes.

"Will, I fainted for you. I've never fainted in my life for anyone or anything. You owe me."

"I do?" He stared at me. "You said yes, or did I imagine it? Did you mean it, Kara?"

My heart hurt with so many feelings bubbling in it, and my eyes burned. "Absolutely, I mean it. Go let the doctors do their work on you. We can figure out the details later."

An exhausted but goofy look came over his face.

"You will?"

I smiled and touched his face again. I wasn't brave

enough to risk whatever he was covered in to actually kiss his cheek.

By now, the EMTs were ready to wheel Will to their vehicle.

I stepped away. "I'll see you there."

Jim and Libbie stood with me as the crews took the stretcher down the rutted road to the vehicles. We turned as one when we heard small noises in the brush and saw Aunt Laura fighting a sticker bush. I rushed to help her, but having made it through the fear, now I had no time for distractions. I was frustrated, thinking this was one more thing to deal with before I could rush after those ambulances and concentrate on Will. My temper was short as Laura asked, "Oh, Kara, what happened to you? You're a sight. Are you hurt? What's that smell? Did you find Will?"

Before I could speak sharply, something unexpected happened. Everything stilled and a calm came over me—a sustaining calm, not the collapsing kind. Businesslike. Seemed almost like my dad had stepped in to do what he did best—set the emotion aside and deal efficiently with what needed attention at the moment.

"Hold still." I gave her a quick, reassuring smile as I untwisted the briars. "There, that's got it."

"Kara, I called your phone over and over, but no one answered. I waited and then I could wait no longer."

"I'll explain in just a moment." I turned to Jim and Libbie. "Thank you both very much."

"Glad you called us."

"Will is planning to get this area cleared, but I don't

think it's a one-man job."

"No worries. He'll have help."

"Good. Whatever it costs. Don't let him scrimp. I knew this place was risky and . . . the result could've been horribly different for him or for someone else."

"Understood."

I was aware of Laura hanging close to me, worried and wanting to know the details. I touched her arm gently to forestall another interruption and said to Jim and Libbie, "I'll go back to the house now and wash up and go to the hospital."

"Walk out to the road with us. We'll drive you over. Both of you, of course."

Laura asked, "The hospital?"

I answered Jim. "No, I need to change first. If I run, the creek path is quicker anyway."

Libbie said, "We'll drive you back to Wildflower so you can change, and then I'll go with you to the hospital."

"Who's in the hospital?" Laura asked. "Is it Will?"

Realizing Laura wouldn't be able to keep up with me on the creek path, I said, "Drive us back to the house, then, and thank you. I can manage getting to the hospital."

Laura said, "Of course she can manage it. I'll be going with her."

And she did. I explained what had happened on the way back to the house, and explained it yet again as we drove from Wildflower to the hospital in Charlottesville.

Somewhere along the way I began to relax, to feel like myself again, but I was grateful to have had that glimpse of my father in myself.

~~~~

Laura said she'd stay in the waiting room, and she hung back while I explained to the woman at the ER desk that I was there for Will Mercer. I let every bit of the urgency I'd experienced back in that clearing show in my voice and in my posture—but with Dad's tightly controlled dignity—and the woman at the desk motioned for me to proceed. As soon as I was through the automatic doors, I heard his voice. He was politely arguing with the doctor—polite, yes, but his voice, even low-key, carried through this world of metal, electronics, and curtains on rings, all the more distinctive because it didn't fit here. And that's essentially what Will was saying. He wanted to go home.

I stood just near the edge of the half-open curtain, listening as the doctor said they preferred he stay overnight for observation. Will said no. He'd been hurt worse. He was healthy. He was going home.

The rings rattled against the metal bar as I grabbed the curtain. Will saw me peeking around it, and the doctor turned to see who his stubborn patient was smiling at.

"You sound better now," I said, stepping around the curtain and close to the foot of the bed.

The doctor gave me a quick, assessing look.

"I'm Kara Hart, Will's fiancée."

The words may not have impressed the doctor overmuch, but Will's face brightened. I noticed a technician of some sort—a woman—give Will an extra-long, perhaps approving glance as she walked by. I moved
~~~~

closer to him.

Will said, “The doc wants me to stay for observation overnight, but I’m going home.”

The doctor said, “The scans were all clear, but he shouldn’t be alone. He *should* stay here, but if he won’t, he needs to have someone watching out for problems that might develop. Plus, I understand he doesn’t live near here, so that’s also a concern.”

“What do you think might happen? A problem related to the head injury or something else?”

“Mostly the head injury. He’s in pain, though, mostly from the ribs. That can be managed better from here for at least tonight.”

“Part of the problem may be the pain and the meds?”

Will said, “Aspirin will work. I’ll be fine.”

“No aspirin,” the doctor said.

I asked, “Can I talk to him privately?”

“Sure. I’ll be back shortly.”

The doctor left us. I stood next to Will. His dark hair looked crazy—almost wildly modern—but mostly as if someone had hosed him down and left the thick locks to dry as they would.

“So, Will, what I see is that you’re sort of being held hostage here in this hospital gown. It’s cute, and it matches your eyes, almost. But the doctor has other considerations, including pain. You forget the accident I was in, and I understand what that kind of trauma can do. Whatever they’ve given you now for the pain is going to wear off. Between administering your own medicine and having that head injury, I understand why they would want you under their care."

He lowered his voice and said softly, "I can't stay here, Kara. If I'm conscious, then I need to be out of here."

"So then, you can't be home alone."

"Okay." He stared straight into my eyes. "I can call my mom. She'll put up with me for a night or two."

I couldn't help myself. My fingers found themselves in his hair, sorting it out and smoothing it down. He had a set of stitches at his temple near his hairline. Much like mine.

He stopped my hand with his own and slid his fingers between mine. Having captured my hand, he held it firmly but carefully, as if he might squeeze too hard, as if I were precious, and that's how we were when the doctor returned.

The doctor cleared his throat and asked, "Will he be in your care?"

Will started to speak, but I cut him off.

"Yes. What symptoms, possible complications, should I watch for?"

The doctor mentioned a few things that might go wrong, but he ended saying that if I was sure and if Will was certain he wanted to take the risk, he'd release him. But he added, "Any question about what you're experiencing, get back here right away."

We all nodded.

"Okay, then, the nurse will be in shortly to review discharge instructions."

He was gone.

When the nurse came in, she brought a pair of scrubs

with her and set them on the bed beside Will. She said, "The clothing you arrived in is bagged, but we won't send you home in the gown." She smiled at him, saying, "These aren't stylish, but they are clean and comfy."

"Thank you," he said.

While Will changed, I waited outside the curtain. It was awfully warm in here, and I was feeling a little flushed. Plus, I felt rather bold at declaring that he'd be staying at Wildflower House.

Why not? I asked myself. He was injured. He needed someone nearby in case . . . Then why did my heart race? I pressed my hand to my chest and told myself to knock off the drama. Just relax. This wasn't about me.

Will pushed the curtain aside. He looked a little lost in those blue scrubs and thick socks and shoe covers. I bit my lip to stop myself from laughing.

He said, "This is proof of how badly I want out of here."

I thought of his injured ribs and reached for the bag. He gripped it more tightly and winced.

I said, "Let me carry it."

"No. I'm not even going to wash these. They're going straight to the landfill."

"Why?"

"It was the nastiest dirt I've ever been in, with decades to marinate. I'm not going to think what's been draining into that pit over the years. No, I'll dig out my wallet, get the important stuff from it, and toss the rest."

"Okay."

A young man showed up with a wheelchair. Will eyed

it, but the young man said, "Required. Doctor said." Will complied. As we exited, I remembered Laura. My aunt was perched on the edge of her seat, looking anxious and frail. When she saw us, she jumped up.

"Oh, Will, look at you. Are you okay?" She rushed toward us.

"Careful," I said. "Bruised ribs."

She stopped and clasped her hands. "I'm glad it's no worse and they are letting you go home."

I said, "They'll only release him to stay with someone because there could be issues, so he's coming home with me."

"Oh," she said again. As we exited to the parking lot, she added, "Does his mother know? I mean, about the accident?"

Will gave a sharp intake of breath and then a soft groan. "Gotta remember not to breathe." He paused, then added, "Probably. I remember telling someone, maybe Jim, to let her know where I was being taken but that I was okay." He added, "Word gets around."

I nodded, only half listening to him, wanting to hurry, to get him home, to where he could rest. And Laura too. She looked exhausted. "Wait here," I said. "I'll bring the car up."

"Deal."

Laura stayed with Will. When I looked back, she was standing next to Will's wheelchair, with the attendant on the other side. And she was holding the bag of dirty clothing. I shook my head and hurried to the car.

As we were driving back, I tried to focus on the road

while watching for hazards, including deer, and keeping an eye on Will too. It was a long drive back in the dark, after a long, stressful day. Will looked uncomfortable. Laura was silent in the back seat.

"Kara."

"Yes, Will?"

"You keep looking over at me. I'll be fine."

"Of course you will."

"I have to call my mother. Make sure she knows what happened. She'll never forgive me if I don't at least try to reach her. Did you bring my phone with you?"

"Oh, goodness. I forgot I had it." I gestured toward my purse, stuck into that space between the front seats. "In there. I dropped your phone in my purse."

Moving gingerly, he checked and found it. "Here it is."

"Okay, call her. Let her know you're with me."

"Thing is . . . when I call her, she'll expect me to . . . you know. And when I explain . . . why I won't . . . she'll speculate."

He was speaking in some weird kind of code, but I understood it was for Laura's sake.

I glanced in the rearview mirror and saw that Laura appeared to be sleeping. Her head was forward and nodding ever so gently.

Softly, I said, "I suppose you could just tell her . . . you know . . . about our plans."

"Yeah? You'd be okay with that? I figured you'd want to discuss how we'll . . . handle things first. As I said before, word gets around, so as soon as that cat is let out of the bag . . ."

"Yes, us talking first would be my preference."

"So . . . I'm inclined to . . . you know . . . go along with her. You won't have to put up with me . . . like this."

"Afraid you'll scare me off?" I laughed softly and very quietly.

"Not going to laugh. Hurts."

He was thumbing at his phone screen. "Oh. She called. She texted too. Text says she's driving to the hospital if she doesn't hear from me soon." He glanced over at me. "That was almost an hour ago."

He dialed. "Mom, I'm fine . . . yes, some stitches, bruised ribs. Nothing much."

I was pretty sure I could hear his mother, Vivi, yelling through the phone.

"Mom, calm down. I'm with Kara. We're on our way back to Cub Creek . . . Yes, going to Wildflower House . . . Wait, there's no need—"

Someone disconnected. Surely it was Vivian. Will looked tired.

I said, "She sounded upset."

"Yeah. She'll calm down. But . . . she's heading to Wildflower House to meet us there and take me home."

My first reaction was to object. But if I'd had a mom who was frantic with worry over me . . .

"Go with her."

"I think we should tell her . . . you know . . . together, but after we've discussed what and how we want . . . it to work. Otherwise, we're inviting a lot of interference, because once we tell anyone, everyone will know, and they love us and they will all have opinions and suggestions."

My circle of friends and family had ballooned practically overnight. I wasn't accustomed to my life being a community project.

"Yes," I said. "I agree." Keeping one hand on the steering wheel, I reached across and took his hand. "Go with her tonight, then come over tomorrow. I'll come pick you up. Spend the day with me and we'll talk."

I sent him a quick smile along with a squeeze of his hand. And then I slowed, barely able to make out my mailbox on this dark country night, and made the turn into the long driveway leading to the house.

I didn't recognize the car parked in front of the house, but I knew it must be Vivian's. Will's sister, Britt, was waiting and watching for us from the front porch.

We exchanged brief greetings. Vivian exclaimed over her son—who topped her by more than a foot and was almost twice as wide—as if he were still a little boy who needed comfort. Maybe he did want comfort. And I—embarrassed though I was to feel this way—felt more like an outsider than a fiancée. I'd never been a mom, but even so I could imagine that for most parents one's children aged in years and appearance but were always and forever their babies.

Will reached toward me, but I said, "Go. I'll come see you tomorrow."

He was mine, and suddenly I was feeling so territorial that I mostly kept my mouth shut because I didn't trust myself not to sound jealous or put out.

Britt got the truck keys from Will, and she drove away first, followed soon by Will and his mother in her car. Laura and I were left standing on the porch, staring out into the quiet February night.

"Aunt Laura, I know you must be exhausted. Why don't you stay here tonight? We'll have a bite to eat and get to bed."

"Do you need me to stay, dear?"

"Need? No. I'm okay."

"Then I'll drive on home. It's dark, but I'll take it easy."

I gave her a smile and a one-armed hug. "How about something to drink first? You're probably dehydrated."

"A glass of tea, maybe?"

"Yes, ma'am."

We went into the house together. I switched on lights as we made our way back to the kitchen. Home, I thought, but someone—an important part of this home—was missing. And I couldn't shake that *missing* feeling. I brought tea and cookies to the table and sat across from Laura. Her eyes were on me and stayed on me.

"Is something wrong, Laura?"

"I think maybe so . . . but maybe not. I'm not a woman of broad experience. Long, maybe"—she paused to smile—"in terms of years, but most of those were spent caring for my mother. My adoptive mother. She was also a loving mother, and I did right by her. Perhaps more right than I should have."

"I don't understand." Truly, I was confused.

"If I'd been smarter, maybe braver, perhaps more

daring . . . I would've found a way to do my duty by my mother and have my own life too. By that, I mean I would've found a way to follow my own dreams without giving up my whole entire life to her needs. Which, in retrospect, I have wondered how much she really needed me. Or was she more afraid of being alone?" She shook her head.

"I'm sorry."

"Oh, no need for that. That's all done and in the past, and look at me now. I have a lovely life. I've found my niece and my brother, Lewis. I need to call him, by the way. Strange how time passes, isn't it?"

"True."

"Plus, I have found the most wonderful friends."

"I feel the same." I was still wondering where all this was coming from.

She fixed me with a bold gaze. "What I'd tell you if you were my daughter would be to pay less attention to what others think or to your own fears—just fight for what you want."

"Fight?"

"For him. If you want him, then go for it."

"Oh. You weren't asleep in the back seat, were you?"

"On and off." She paused for a sip of tea. "Missed opportunities are just that—missed. Life occasionally gives us do-overs. A husband and a wife must commit to put each other first. Everyone else who loves you will fall in line to support you. If they don't . . . well, that tells its own story, doesn't it?"

I stood and walked around the table to where she

stood. I put my arms around her. She was about my height but seemed shorter, maybe because she was so thin, and felt almost frail when I hugged her.

In a teasing voice, I said, "I'll tell you a secret, if you promise not to share."

Laura smiled sweetly. "I already know, dear Kara. I just want you to stop fretting over the details. Focus on yourself and Will. Even things that seem so important . . . Sometimes we're so worried about managing everything responsibly that one day we look up and discover that the world and everyone else has moved on. Don't be that person, Kara—the left-behind one. Take a chance."

She took my hand. "Let's make a promise to each other. You can trust me to keep your secret"—she gave a little laugh—"such as it is. And I'll trust you to actually enjoy the many blessings you've received. If you do, I can absolutely promise you that you'll be better prepared to deal with the disappointments."

Chapter Seven

Three days after Valentine's Day ~

The next morning, I was waiting again—this time for Will to call or text and tell me to come fetch him. I was ready to drive over. But no one contacted me. I understood he was probably hurting more than he'd expected. If so, I'd go over and keep him company there, for at least a while. Surely his mother wouldn't mind.

Back in December, Vivi Mercer had joined us for Christmas dinner at Wildflower House. A very nice lady who, in return, had invited me to her family get-together on New Year's Day. Everyone was nice, but we were all still new to each other. I didn't want to make things more difficult or inconvenient for her or anyone else, but I needed to see how Will was doing—in person.

It was midmorning already. How much longer must I wait?

A vehicle arrived outside. *Will?*

I jumped up from Dad's chair and ran to the door.

It was Sue Deale. Her husband was seated in the driver's side of the truck, and Sue was coming up the steps. She saw me at the storm door and waved. She was using a cane. And a big bow was tied to it near the top.

I opened the door. "Good morning, Sue. Surprised to see you. Are you okay?"

She followed my gaze and saw I was staring at her cane. She laughed and handed it to me.

"Sue?"

She'd turned aside, bending to pick up a pot of something from the bench. It was a stainless-steel, copper-bottomed pot with a lid on it. I leaned the cane against the wall and hurried out to help Sue with the pot and was glad I did because it was heavy.

"Careful," she said. "It's still hot. Potato soup."

She yelled over toward the truck, "Bring that bread up here, would you?" Facing me again, she said in a normal voice, "I nearly forgot that bread. Would've been a shame, for sure."

Her husband did indeed join us on the porch with the bread wrapped in a colorful dish towel. He offered it to me, saying, "Ma'am," and then hurried back to his truck.

Sue shook her head. "He isn't much for words, but he's handy. I'll say that for him."

I held the door open for her to enter.

Sue Deale knew everything and everyone that in any way related to this region. I was convinced of that. Sue was like the community glue that kept things together and functioning, with or without our agreement. Which is exactly why I wasn't all that surprised when she said, "Potato soup is Will's favorite. Made that sourdough bread for him too. Man like him needs bracing food to recover."

She stared at me, waiting, but I was still digesting the idea of the cane, the soup, and the bread. She prompted, "Shall I take it back to the kitchen?"

"Certainly. Thank you."

I followed, warning myself to be careful of what I said or asked. Sue would either intuit everything on my mind or drive me to confess it all, and then it would be like an open missive going straight out into the universe for all to receive. And to comment on. And add to the information . . . So if I didn't want something shared, I needed to have the smarts and the self-discipline not to speak the words aloud.

I followed. "Sue, this is so kind of you. Shall I take this over to Vivian's house for Will?"

"Oh my." She gaped for a fraction of a moment. "Isn't he headed over here? That's what I heard. Though, for the life of me, I don't know why you'd want that. Nothing more aggravating than a sick or injured man. Truly. Believe me, I know." She shook her head. "The only thing worse is one that's on the mend and feeling well enough to be a nuisance."

I tried to look open, innocent of juicy information, as if I was only waiting for her to continue.

She frowned a little. "I'm certain that Vivi said Britt was bringing him over."

"Oh? That's good. They haven't called. Not that I'm complaining. I suspect they've had their hands full with helping Will?"

Sue laughed. "Well, I guess you'll see. When I heard,

I said to Joe that I'd better carry some healing food over to Kara."

A smile forced its way out. "Healing food?"

"Potato soup, like I said."

"Isn't that chicken soup?"

"Oh goodness. You aren't telling me he has a cold too, does he?"

"Oh, no cold. Not as far as I know."

"Well, we'll all be thankful for that."

She walked up the hallway back toward the front door. "You let me know if you need anything. I'm not far."

The cane was leaning against the wall next to the door. She picked it up and handed it to me again. "This is for Will. Tell him I offer it with my best wishes for a speedy recovery."

"I will."

Having brought news and provisions, she climbed up into the truck, riding off to do good deeds with her handy husband.

I stared at the cane with its gaily painted parrot head and a red bow.

Would Will find it as amusing as I did? I didn't even care that it sparked memories of when I had needed a cane. As for the potato soup, I suspected he'd welcome that. Sue would know, wouldn't she? She seemed to know most everything about everyone.

He could have the cane, but the soup and fresh bread? That he'd have to share.

~~~~
~~~~

Soon after Sue left, Laura arrived, walking in with a cheery, “Good morning.” She asked, “What smells so good?” And then continued straight back to the kitchen, following her nose. She returned quickly. “Is that Sue’s potato soup?”

“It is.”

“She’s famous for it, you know.” Laura squinted, questioning. “Why did she bring it?”

“Will’s on his way, so I’ve heard.”

She smiled and nodded. “Well, then. That’s good. We’ll be happy to see him, and I’m glad he’s up to the trip. That must be a very good sign of recovery. Meanwhile, dear, I’ll get back to work. I’ll have information for you to review later today.” She added, “You let me know if you need help with anything.” With a light step, she walked away, stepped into the project room, and gently closed the door.

Okay, I thought.

And because I was standing there, wondering at the sometimes puzzling and mysterious people I seemed to attract, I heard another vehicle drive up and stop in front of the house.

It was Will’s truck this time. His sister, Britt, was driving. She slid down from the high seat, landing carefully on her good leg. She was still favoring her injured leg. She wore a brace on it, and that surely made certain movements awkward for her. She, too, understood pain.

I was on the porch now, and she glanced at me with a sour expression on her face as she limped around to the passenger side to reach the door before Will tried to climb out alone, but he glowered at her and said, "Stay back."

Maybe it was the patient and not the pain that made Britt look so irritable.

We met on the stairs. She said, "I brought him over myself so he wouldn't even think about driving himself home."

"Thank you. I'll get him back to your mom's place later."

"Good enough," she said. She handed me a small envelope. "His pain pills. He's allowed three a day. He's already had one. He should take them with food." She put them into my hands. "His ribs are wrapped. Not sure if that actually does any good, since they're bruised but not broken. At the very least, though, it should help remind him to protect them, to take it easy."

"Got it."

"Yeah? Well, good luck. He's an awful patient. Maybe he'll use his better manners with you."

Will was clearly ignoring his sister. He was focused on reaching the front steps.

"Thank you, Britt. I'll let you know when he's coming back."

She shook her head and waved goodbye. I turned to follow Will.

~~~~

"No need to treat me like a baby," he said and winced as he grasped the railing.
~~~~

"No need at all." I opened the door, and he stepped slowly across the porch to the threshold.

"I'm slow but whole. And my brain is still working, as far as I know."

"You are grumpy. Do you want to go back with Britt? I can call her. She won't have gotten far."

"Not funny. Just give me a chance to catch my breath. To sit for a bit. That truck . . . I had no idea what a rough ride it has." After a long moment of breathing, he said, in a more Will-like tone, "They hover. They mean well. I remember how it was when Britt's leg was broken so badly. She needed help, but we tended to suffocate her. Now it's my turn, I guess, but I don't like it." He took another long moment to breathe. "And I'm not hurt that bad. Nothing broken, even. Just bruising."

I let the complaints and excuses pass me by. I saw the paleness around his mouth and eyes. The thin layer of perspiration around his hairline. I noted the stitches in his hairline near his temple and held myself back from touching my own scar. My accident had been . . . what? Almost three years ago? And yet it was recent enough for me that just seeing Will experience this brought my own limp back.

"I'll get us something to drink."

I fetched myself a glass of fruit water and sweet tea for Will and took them back to the sitting room and set them on the small table between the two chairs. One chair was traditionally mine. The other had been Dad's. It fit Will fine. He didn't associate it with my father since they'd met only briefly, and he seemed to find it comfy. I situated myself in my chair, sitting back but leaning on the chair's arm toward him.

"I think we should talk, if you're up to it. While we're here and uninterrupted . . . I almost forgot. Laura is here. She is, however, shut in the workroom. I believe she's making phone calls."

"Shut in the workroom?"

"By her choice. She's enjoying working on the graphics and getting info about what we need for the website. Honestly, I'd hardly put my folder with what I'd already gathered into her hands and the very next day she was doing ad mock-ups. Can you believe it? Plus, I wasn't the most inviting companion this morning."

"Nor I." He tried to breathe deeply, realized his mistake and winced and frowned, then put his head back.

"Then we'll just keep our voices down, okay?"

He gave me a sideways look. "You aren't taking it back, are you?"

"My 'I will'?" I shook my head. "Not a chance."

He turned his head to face me full-on. "Okay, then. Tell me."

"Our engagement . . . we should discuss how we'll announce it. And the things people will ask us. Like when and where and so on."

Again, he looked askance, a little cagey. He reached up to rake his fingers through his hair as if to get it out of his face, and he winced again. "Ouch," he said.

"Will, please stop acting as if I'm about to dash your dreams and break your heart. It's very annoying."

"Yes, ma'am. Just be sure to take good care of it."

"Of what?"

"My heart, Kara."

"We'll make that promise to each other—but the question is when, and how we move toward that point."

"All business."

I smiled. "For now. Who knows how long before someone else comes walking in that front door?"

"Yes."

"So, for instance, how long an engagement did you have in mind?"

This time, he leaned forward, or started to, then settled back in the chair with a low groan.

Worried, I moved nearer. "What's wrong? I mean, has anything changed from what you're already experiencing? The doctor said to watch for that."

He sighed. "No, I am merely disappointed."

I frowned. "What? With me?"

"No, with these ribs. They are definitely taking me off my game."

Raising my eyebrows, I asked, "You have game?"

"Oh, yes, ma'am, I do. Just wait until I'm better. I'll prove it."

"I'll look forward to that."

"As for the engagement and details, I want what you want, Kara. However long or short. You name it. How we announce it? You name it. I do have ideas, but I want to hear your preference first. If I disagree, it won't be hard to change my mind. I'm inclined to be obliging."

Inclined to be obliging. There he went again, dropping those surprising lines when I least expected it.

This was less descriptive than *a preponderance of pines* and was probably some archaic phrase. I couldn't remember when anyone had ever said to me that they were *inclined to be obliging.* It had a medieval feel, I thought. Or maybe like something out of Jane Austen.

"I am likewise inclined, Will. I think we should move straight to marriage."

His expression went blank. He stared at me.

Quickly, I added, "If you truly want an engagement period . . . say six months or a year . . . I'm open to considering it, but I'm more inclined to move forward." I shrugged, saying, "I happen to know that in Virginia there's no waiting period. We could go to the courthouse, get a license, and get married right then and there. We might need to make an appointment first." I left it there, sat back, and waited for Will to speak.

His expression darkened. He looked aside. I kept my mouth shut, but now I was feeling anxious again.

"How do you just happen to know that?"

I shrugged. "I was on the computer and searched on it a few days ago."

"A few days ago? You were intending to say yes even then." He half frowned, then mumbled something while looking down at his sling as if ready to curse it.

"Will?" I whispered.

"I'm hampered, Kara. Hampered. I can't . . . participate very well. I'd told myself that in a month I'd be over this. I'd be good as new. But as it is . . ."

I grinned. "What exactly is it that you need to participate in?"

His cheeks flushed, and the blue in his eyes darkened almost to violet. I was entranced. Meanwhile, whatever conversation going on in his head seemed to conclude, and he nodded.

I said, "As long as you can stand and say, 'I do', then you can handle your part in the ceremony. In fact, even standing isn't required. As for the rest, a marriage doesn't last one night. Those details will work themselves out."

He stared at me. "You're a deep thinker. Kind of scary, actually." He sighed, but in a slow, controlled way that minimized his wincing. "Next steps, then. What do we do first? Tell my mother, I think. Yes."

"Will it offend her? That we're basically eloping?"

"She'll get over it."

A long, very silent pause fell between us until I said, "She'll want to be there. I suppose she could. Your sister too."

He said, "But even just inviting them to go along with us to the courthouse . . . How could we do that without inviting Laura and Lewis? They're family too." He coughed lightly, then winced again.

I left my chair and went to kneel beside him. I took his hand. "Will, we can wait. Maybe we *should* wait. You do need time to recover."

He squeezed my hand. "I don't know. Kara, I'm not a *signs* kind of guy, but everywhere I've gone over the past few weeks, I hear something about how *time doesn't wait* or *don't put things off*. Maybe falling into that hole and having to get fished out of it with heavy equipment sort of put an exclamation mark on it for me. I had no idea that you'd be willing to get married immediately. I'd consoled myself that it would be okay if you wanted a long engagement because it would give me time to heal. But for me? As far as I'm concerned, let's get married this afternoon and to heck with the rest of them. I can get well later."

I'd been seeing and hearing those signs myself. Neither of us was superstitious or particularly imaginative in that way, so it seemed to me that we should pay all the more attention. In fact, at this moment, I was feeling grateful for them. I laughed and pressed the back of his hand to my cheek.

"So let's do some thinking together. If we include your mom and sister, and my aunt and uncle, then who are we leaving out? I want it small, but I don't want to hurt anyone."

"What about Nicole and Mel? Maddie, of course."

"As a flower girl? Yes, even a small, private wedding can have a flower girl." I sighed. "Victoria too. I'll need to invite her. She'll never understand if I don't. And frankly, I think I'd like her to be there."

"Feels right, Kara. Good instincts."

Something about his words—his approval? No, not that, but the support, the sound in his voice that said he knew I'd always figure it out and that he trusted me.

"Kara." He leaned a fraction toward me despite the pain. He lifted my face. "What's wrong? Why are you crying?"

"I'm not," I said as I brushed the wetness from my cheeks. "I'm not crying. I'm happy. And scared. This is feeling very real."

Somehow, his arm on his good side went around my back and tugged me upward. I had to help to settle on his thigh, and I balanced there carefully, leaning into his good side.

I whispered, "Are you sure, Will? Are you ready to take this on? I can't promise it will work, that I can live up to your vision of what you want our marriage to be."

He brushed his lips against my hair and my ear, whispering back, "Nor can I. But frankly, it's worth the risk. I'd rather fail with you than succeed with anyone else."

"You say that now, but—" I broke off, but my distress showed before I could hide it. When I was back in control, I said, "I'm sorry. I know you're in pain. Now I'm going to get up, and I'll move very carefully. When I do, what can I get you? Something more to drink? To eat?"

"Sure." He touched my cheek again. "I'm due for one of those pills again, so something to eat and drink with it would be good. Maybe some of that potato soup? After that, we can resume this discussion. Our planning . . . our future."

"I'll be right back." I left, taking a strange feeling with me. Emotional responses—when they escaped my control—didn't distress Will in the way they'd affected my father. As a child, I'd learned to withhold expressing overt emotion because Dad would shut down, drawing into himself, unable to deal with it. Will was different. Not necessarily yielding to the emotion, but accepting of it.

I returned with food and found Laura sitting with

Will. She was holding the folder I'd given her. Her purse was on the floor beside her feet. She stood when she saw me.

"I'll take this material home to work on, if you don't mind?"

"I don't mind at all. Is there anything else you need?"

"No, this should do for this afternoon. I've made some calls and written notes, but I want to pull them all together and find the gaps and all that. I hope you don't mind that I won't have it ready for you today."

"Not at all. Thank you, Laura."

She shook her head. "Thank you." With a sudden, excited look, she smiled at the both of us and whispered happily, "Congratulations, you two." And she left.

Will said, "You told her?"

"As a secret," I said. "She wasn't surprised, but she *was* pleased."

I set the mug of soup with the buttered bread on the side on the table.

Will said, "The *where* is the simplest question of all."

"Wildflower House? Not the courthouse?"

"Yes. It feels right. Would you mind if our pastor officiates? I admit I don't make it to church every Sunday, but it's part of my life, and I've known him for as far back as I can remember. Any objection? And regardless of whether he officiates, I know he'd like to meet you. Do you mind?" After a moment of silence, he added, "I heard you, you know. Praying for me to be rescued."

I'd been speaking aloud? Apparently so. "I meant it, Will."

"It helped me…down in that…place. Thank you."

"As for meeting your pastor and him officiating, I'm fine with that." I patted his arm. "What else? What about the honeymoon?"

Will picked up the mug and breathed in the aroma of the soup. "That's easy too. Wherever you are, Kara, that's where I'll be."

~~~~

Will dozed midway through his soup. It was a brief snooze, and I was nearby when he woke.

"Kara?"

"I'm here."

"Did I doze off? Sorry."

"Not a problem."

He said, "Good. I have to confess something to you."

"Okay."

"You can't get too angry with me because you already told Laura. I told my mom last night."

"Oh."

"Had to. She brought it up. She wasn't surprised either." He looked around, dissatisfied with something.

"What's wrong, Will?"

"Please pull up a chair. Maybe a dining room chair? Sit close."

I did as he asked. I sat and then scooted the chair even closer, so that my knees were between his, touching the chair cushion he was sitting on. I leaned still farther forward and asked, "What's wrong?"
~~~~

He offered a grin, but it didn't light up his face like his pre-injury grins had done.

"So, this is the thing. I told Mom I'd proposed."

"Oh."

"She promised to keep it quiet until we give her permission to share." He fidgeted with his pocket, trying to grab something.

I reached to help him, but he stayed my hand with his.

"Patience, please. I'm slow. This is not how I planned it." He retrieved a small blue velvety case. My heart stopped.

His face was suddenly flushed. "When I told her, she asked me to give this to you, if you're willing to wear it. It was my grandmother's and great-grandmother's too. Mom kept it in a safe-deposit box at the bank, so I guess she was expecting the proposal to happen soon since she got it out to have ready for us."

Still holding the small case, he said, "I would never have chosen a ring for you without knowing your preferences. I'd imagined we'd do that together. And we still can. This ring can be a promise, a temporary promise in advance of the real thing. Please know that. And never in a million years did I think I would slip a ring onto your finger while sitting back in a chair and not down on my knee. I hope you'll forgive me for that."

He tried to lean forward, and the color drained from his face. I saw how much it hurt him to hold back the groan. I put my hands around his.

"Will, this doesn't have to happen today. But there's also no reason it can't happen today. This is you and me,

Will. We don't have to follow anyone else's examples or traditions. We can make our own."

Will put his head back again. He whispered, "I hope you mean that. Seems like we've taken our own path right from the beginning, doesn't it? Well, this will be very different too. I want to give this to you now because I took that pill and I'll probably fall asleep, and when I wake up, with the pain more manageable, I'll make my way out to your car, and we'll drive to my mother's house, and we'll *officially* tell her together. Are you okay with that?"

"I am."

"Good." He opened the box and pulled out a beautiful ring—a sapphire ringed with small diamonds. "This was my father's mother's ring. Mom said that Dad wanted me to have this for my bride. Will you be my wife, Kara? Will you marry me?"

My face felt hot. Flushed. My eyes felt teary again. "I will."

I offered my hand, holding it close to him, and he slipped the ring on my finger. He looked up and smiled at me, then pulled my hand to his lips and kissed the back. He held my hand for a long moment, then said, "I'm sorry, but I think it's nap time, Kara."

Touching his face gently, I smoothed his hair back and away from his stitches. I moved my chair aside and pushed the hassock up close and lifted his feet onto it, then pulled the throw from the sofa.

"Take a nap, Will. I'm going to call Victoria."

He mumbled, "Good idea," and closed his eyes.

CHAPTER EIGHT

Leaving Will, I walked quietly down the hall to the kitchen and dialed Victoria's phone number. She answered right away.

"Hello, Vic. How are you?"

"Fine? Sorry, but you sound odd."

"Will is napping. He—"

"There? At Wildflower? What's up?"

"Wait. I'll explain. Just take a breath and give me a chance."

"You were fine when we spoke a few days ago. What happened, Kara?"

I could see her hunting for her purse and keys, ready to dash out of wherever she was and race here to Wildflower.

"I'm fine. Will's fine. We're *all* fine. But we have news."

"We? You have *news* and *everything's* good," she repeated after me, then she squeaked. "You're *engaged.* I knew it! I'm so happy for both of you!"

"Good guess. And yes, we are."

Her words spilled out of the phone in a gushing rush.

"Have you set the date yet? It'll be at Wildflower House, right? Just imagine—the first bridal event there will be yours."

"Calm down. There's more."

"What? Tell me."

"It's going to be a very short engagement."

"What?" She whispered, "You aren't . . . are you?"

"No. Definitely not. I just don't see any sense in waiting. We know we want to get married, and I don't want a big ceremony, so there's no planning to speak of."

"Hmm. Are you sure?"

"I'm sure, and Will agrees with me."

"He agrees with you because that's what you want."

"Isn't that what I said?"

"Not quite."

I was annoyed now. "Well, that's what we've decided to do, so I was calling you because—"

She interrupted, "That's fine. It's just different when you live where everybody knows everybody. But that's fine, if that's what y'all want."

"You don't know this, but Will was injured yesterday. Fell into a pit, and it could've ended up far worse than it did, but he has stitches and bruised ribs, so . . ."

"*Whoa*. He's okay?"

"He will be."

"Then why not wait a month so he can actually say *I do* without looking pained about it?"

I was silent.

"Guess he doesn't want to wait?"

Well, he was willing to. But still I stayed silent.

Victoria said, somewhat more gently, "I can see I'm needed. I'll be there for supper. Not taking no for an answer, so don't bother saying it. Do you have food, or should I bring something?"

"Rather presumptuous."

"Yes, I am. Always have been. Shall we say six o'clock? Am I bringing for two or three?"

I let it go and rolled with it. "Just the two of us. He'll be back at his mom's by then."

"Okay."

"He wants to be here. I want him to be here. But his mom . . ."

"Shared care situation?" She laughed. "No matter, soon you'll have full custody." She laughed again, then settled down. "No worries, Kara. Things work out. Experience has taught us that, hasn't it? Let me get my work finished so my employer doesn't give me a hard time when I leave early. See you later."

And she was gone. I hadn't even had the chance to ask her to be my maid of honor. Small wedding, limited to close family, but Victoria had been my past and present. Both friend *and* enemy at certain times. Almost a sister, in many ways. She was the natural person for me to ask. And as reluctant as I might be to admit it, I needed a fresh bucket of energy and optimism in addition to the one with common sense.

~~~~

Just getting Will into the vehicle and watching for road
~~~~

issues that might cause bumps was exhausting and didn't leave a lot of room for worried imaginings. I stood by the car as he worked his way out of the vehicle, and his mother came out to the porch.

"He's very sore."

"I'm sure," she said, and she glanced at my hand. But she didn't smile or even congratulate us. I pretended not to notice, but it did hurt a little.

I stayed close to him as he climbed the four steps up to the front door of his mother's home. He waved her aside and crossed the threshold alone. When I hesitated, she touched my arm and said, "Please do come inside."

The living room wasn't huge, but it was neat and cozy. The recliner was front and center, and Will made his way there slowly. Seeing him move like that, so far from his usual energy and joy of life, I knew we'd have to make a slight alteration in our plans. He was going to need more time to heal. Pushing him to do too much too quickly didn't make sense. And yet . . .

While he was easing himself down into the chair, I asked, "May I?" He nodded. I turned to Vivian and said, "Thank you so much for offering us this beautiful ring, this family treasure. I appreciate your thoughtfulness. Your kindness." Impulsively, I added, "Your trust."

She shook her head, looking almost miserable. I felt my own brave expression dim. She caught my hand.

"Please don't think my . . . reticence? Whatever this is that I'm feeling . . . has anything to do with the actual fact of you and Will getting married. There's no guarantee about any marriage, and Will wants this, and if you do too, then I'm one hundred percent behind you."

She seemed to run out of steam, then rallied. "There is no parent in the world who, when told their child is getting married, doesn't have . . . who isn't assailed by memories, good and bad, of their own days of falling in love, of living in that glow until life begins . . . to interfere. It is a joyful but also a bittersweet feeling." She reached out and took my hands. "I want the absolute best for both of you. Now help me shake off this swampy feeling . . . Grandma Mercer always called it *malaise*. For me, it just feels bittersweet, and I'd like to focus on the sweet. What have you two decided to do about the wedding? How long an engagement do you have planned?"

"Short," Will said.

"Short," I said, but I added, "Maybe allowing a week or two for Will to heal a little."

"We don't have to wait," he said. He sounded annoyed.

Vivian and I looked at each other. She understood and jumped in, saying, "Actually, that's a good idea." She cast a quick glance at me, and I nodded. "Even a small wedding needs some planning. This will be your one and only . . ." The sentence trailed off as she looked at me again, this time saying, "I'm sorry, Kara, I didn't mean to imply that it meant less for you because . . ."

"No, it's okay. I understand." I tossed Will a quick, reassuring smile and touched Vivian's hand. "We'll figure out the details later, but for today, I think he's had enough."

I touched his forehead and worried that he felt warm.

I kissed his cheek lightly despite his mother standing over us.

"Kara, I'll see you tomorrow."

"Tomorrow, Will."

I left then. I felt unsettled. As if I'd left a crucial part of my life behind.

That old "thinking too much" habit wouldn't shut up as I drove back to Wildflower House. It had been awkward with Vivian, but she hadn't done anything wrong. To her, and perhaps to others, Will and I looked like a mismatch. Love didn't always conquer all. In fact, love rarely triumphed over the realities of daily life and wayward hearts. But that was my experience with Niles, not with Will. And yet anyone looking at us would think Niles and I were the right match, not me and Will. Then I heard Laura's voice telling me not to sweat the details. And I remembered that Victoria was driving out from Richmond and bringing food and conversation.

Victoria was Victoria. She often had good ideas. She was impulsive, sometimes over-the-top, but always enthusiastic, even in her mistakes and despite the wreckage she sometimes left behind.

But the good counted too.

There was a lot about Victoria that I admired. Except when those same traits drove me crazy.

And thinking that, I smiled.

~~~~

Victoria arrived with a flourish, the storm door swinging as she shouted my name. "Kara, I'm here. Kara? Where
~~~~

are you?" Her voice echoed up the hallway.

She would've seen right off that I wasn't in the sitting room or the parlor, and her footsteps coming up the long hallway toward the kitchen were unmistakable.

I called out, "In the kitchen."

She emerged from the dark hallway and into the well-lit kitchen, where I was pulling out plates and drinking glasses.

"What'd you bring?" I asked.

"Lasagna from that fabulous Italian restaurant in Short Pump. Figured we'd need to reheat it anyway." She set the bag on the counter, and yes, the smell was utterly charming. I closed my eyes and breathed in, suddenly realizing how hungry I was.

She added, "Microwave will work."

I pulled out the salad makings, and we washed our hands and went to work on the assembly.

"Talk," she said. "Tell me."

As I trimmed the celery, I said, "*Marriage*. So much is rolled up into that one word."

"True."

"He wants to. I want to. I was worried about making a mistake that would hurt us both, but him falling into that hole on the Lange property superseded all other concerns."

"Fixed your thinking?"

"Yes. Showed me . . . well, it's something Will himself said. I'd rather fail at marriage with him than succeed with anyone else."

"Wow. Smart guy. Super romantic, but I do see flaws in that statement."

"I'm sure you do." I grunted. "As do I. And I do have concerns."

"Because you're sane. Because this isn't your first go-round. It's always easier when you're ignorant of how badly things can go."

"At least you have insight into my problem. Now I must overcome it. I want to move forward, with Will."

"So, you said yes."

"I have."

She'd been eying my hand, and now she grabbed it. "Gorgeous! Family heirloom?"

"Yes. Will's grandmother's ring. Maybe his great-grandmother's too."

"Nice. Very nice." After a close look, she released my hand. "What were you saying about the wedding date? Why the rush to the altar?"

"Not a rush, but why wait? Will and I know what we want."

By now we had the salad mixed, and I stopped the microwave to check the lasagna, found it steaming, and we put it all on the table as Victoria was saying, "So the sooner the better because you're afraid you'll talk yourself out of it? Run away before reaching the altar?"

"No. Why would I do that?" I sat in my chair at the table. "Yes. I might. Not run, but I'll torture myself and everyone around me until I get there." I was forlorn.

"Then your focus is wrong."

I just looked at her.

"Sure. If you've said yes, and you're committed, then your focus should be on the wedding and your life together after. Whether you get married tomorrow or next month, planning for *after* should be enough to keep you from fretting yourself to death. If you are still fretting, then maybe the commitment isn't sincere."

I gaped, gathered my cool, and said, "I'm sincere. I love Will. He loves me. I said yes."

"Well, just sayin' . . . if you're going to bolt, then you need to tell him now because you both deserve better than that kind of last-minute soap-opera drama."

"No, I couldn't do that."

"Well, then, stop gnawing on it over and over." She laughed. "Do I know you or what?"

I sighed.

"So when?"

"We were going for right away, as in *now*. I suggested we go to the justice of the peace and say the words and sign on the dotted line."

"You could, but yuck. Not much celebration happening there."

I ignored her opinion of my idea. I said, "But I do think we should also include his mother and sister, and then there's Laura and Lewis. So I think a small ceremony. That being the case, I'm thinking Wildflower House. Will prefers that too. And seeing how much pain Will is in, I'm thinking of maybe waiting a week, at most two, to let him get past the worst of the pain."

Her eyes had widened. If Victoria could look shocked, she did at that moment. Quickly, she covered her mouth with her napkin, as if in her shock she was going to spray lasagna and salad across the table.

"Seriously, Victoria? Are you ten?"

"No, but maybe *you* are." With extreme sarcasm, she said, "How kind of you to give him the chance to get over the worst of the pain."

"He can recover here after we're married." I shrugged. "For that matter, he could've recovered here from the start, but his mother had other ideas."

"Honestly, Kara, sometimes I wonder. For such a smart person . . ." She shook her head, then said slowly, "So is there so little difference between being married and not married that it's just something you get around to when it's convenient? Will's a pretty serious guy. He knows that something a person does when it's convenient is just as easily undone when it becomes inconvenient."

"Marriage and commitment aren't necessarily the same thing."

"They should be. For Will, I think they are."

I chewed, thinking on it. There was value here in being able to express myself so boldly—to work out these thoughts—even if Victoria was sometimes momentarily rude in her reactions.

She said, "So maybe a month out? That would give you time to plan."

"A month? For a small, private wedding?"

"Hmm. Okay, let's think this through." Her fingers went up one by one as she named them. "Will and you. Vivian and Britt. Laura and Lewis. Lewis's daughter, because she's your cousin and will probably come along with him. Maddie Lyn, right? She'll expect to be your flower girl, whether you think you need one or not, and you'd better not consider doing without, or you'll have to answer to me." She pointed her fork in my direction, as if making a point.

"Yes, agreed about Maddie Lyn."

"But then how can you leave out her grandmother, Mel, and Nicole?" She ran out of fingers and simply spread her hands wide to show as much.

My voice had gotten softer, lower, as the count increased. "I can't."

Victoria nodded. "What about Will? Is there a good friend? A school friend or coworker that he'll want? You might be able to exclude his cousins, maybe, if he has a bunch of them, but he must have a close male friend he'll want to stand up with him?"

"I don't know. Probably. I've met a couple of his friends. They seemed fine. He's lived in this area his whole life."

"Well, then."

"Well, then."

She leaned toward me. "But don't worry, Kara. We can still keep it simple and low-key. I promise you that. If you tell me what you want, I'll handle the logistics. You know I can. And while you'd hate having to wrangle the details, I'll love doing it, won't I?"

"Yes, you will."

She grinned, big and bold. Proud. "And that's why you called me, right?"

I shook my head slowly. "No. Actually, I called to ask if you'd stand up with me, as my maid of honor."

Victoria jumped to her feet, sending the chair flying

backward. She rushed around the table to hug me, saying, “I will. I will.”

She tugged me out of my seat and pulled me from the kitchen. I cast one look back at the half-eaten food and the dirty dishes on the counter as Victoria said, “Keep up. Stick with me, here, Kara. We’re going to replace all those whirling dervish worries in your head with better things to think about.”

She pulled me into the wide doorway of the sitting room. She waved her arm, pointing as she went, at the parlor opposite, the broad foyer, the dining room next to us, and then she waved at all those spaces at once, including the grand staircase. “See this, Kara. We have chairs in the sitting room and foyer. Music coming from the parlor. A champagne fountain or maybe a chocolate fountain working its magic in the dining room next to an amazing wedding cake. And then . . . and then . . . the tune strikes up and Will comes up the hallway to stand just inside the parlor with his best man and the pastor. And then, and then, and then . . . *down* the stairs you come. A beautiful dress. I don’t see you in a wedding cake dress, but something classic and slim and elegant, with Maddie Lyn ahead of you and me right behind you. You come down the stairs, pausing ever so slightly at the last step, then turning this way toward your guests and Will.” She was still holding on to me, but she pressed her free hand to her heart. “You take his breath away. His eyes . . .”

“Enough.”

“Are you sure?”

“Yes.”

"Because I've captured your attention, right? You're seeing the vision I'm painting?"

I bit my lip. "Maybe."

"Yes! I knew it." She tugged my hand. "Remember, all of this is merely a suggestion. You make all the final decisions."

"Yes."

"Okay. Next." She pulled my hand, tugging on my arm too hard.

"Hey, ouch."

"Oh, come on. Don't be a baby." And with that encouragement, she all but dragged me up the stairs. I struggled to keep up.

She led me down the hall to my bedroom at the back of the house, and we stopped in the doorway. She pointed an accusing finger at my room and said, "No."

"No?"

"This won't work."

"What won't work? I chose this room so I could look out the window and see the wildflowers and the creek beyond."

"That was then. This is now. We are thinking of *now* now. You chose this room to see the wildflowers and to leave the big, fancy front room for your father. The wildflowers are gone . . ." She broke off.

"And Dad is too."

As if planned, we shared a moment of silence before Victoria spun back into action.

"Back to *now*," she said as she guided me back up the hallway to the front of the house. "This would probably be obvious to most people, but you are so stubborn and pigheaded that I'm not assuming it's true for you."

"Don't be insulting."

"I'm not. Your tunnel vision is also one of your charms, but in this case, I'm making sure it doesn't get in the way of you achieving what you want."

We now stood just inside the door to my father's room.

She moved her hand again with sweeping gestures at the tall front windows in the turret area, then the long, unbroken stretch of wall where the mahogany bedposts showed off their intricate carvings, and toward the brand-new bathroom that I'd just had installed. I'd had this room painted in shades of silver-gray and cool blues with white trim. A grand, serene room intended for paying guests.

Victoria said, "Your marriage deserves this room. Your husband and you deserve this room."

"But guests . . ."

"Not currently here. We are dealing in *now*." She shook her head. "Besides, you never intended Wildflower to be an actual bed-and-breakfast, did you? You have four other gorgeous bedrooms, just not as nice as this one."

"But—"

"Don't, Kara. Will should know how important this marriage, this commitment, is to you. Words aren't good enough. Don't misunderstand me. Words are important, but they can also be empty, easily changed, and oft forgotten. Show him. Welcome him into your home and into your life with so much joy and fanfare that he can't . . ." Her voice faded away, and now she was looking into some distance I couldn't discern. "He won't ever wonder if he truly belongs here with you."

"Victoria? Are you okay?"

She nodded. "I'm fine. Just had a moment. Like déjà vu in reverse." She squeezed my hand and turned toward me. "I've met someone, Kara. He's so great. He thinks . . . or says he thinks . . . that I'm great too. This might be the real thing. If it is, Kara, if *he* is, then I'm going to remember everything I just said to you when *our* time comes."

I squeezed her hand this time. "I'd like to meet him. I hope you'll bring him to the wedding."

She blushed.

With a smile, I added, "There's always room for one more, especially *your* plus one."

CHAPTER NINE

Almost a week after Valentine's Day ~

There was still room for another one plus one when Jim called four days after the accident. By then I'd given up counting. We were dealing in estimates now.

But when the phone rang, the noises coming from the foyer weren't conducive to conversation, so I asked him, "Can you hold a minute, Jim?"

"Sure."

I stuck my head in the workroom and told Laura, "I'll be back. It's a little noisy out here with the piano tuner, and I want to take this call. Shall I close the door for you?"

"Piano tuner?" Jim asked.

I grinned. "One more minute, Jim."

Laura nodded. I closed the door gently behind me and walked on to the kitchen.

"Sorry about that. Sometimes Wildflower House gets like this. Crazy with life. The piano tuner arrived this morning. He drove over from Richmond. I don't know how much longer he'll be at it, but that's okay. It'll be worth it." I didn't stop in the kitchen but walked out to the back porch, saying, "I'm glad you called, because I wanted to speak with you."

Jim said, "If it's about clearing your grandparents' property, we had a job fall off the schedule."

He'd called it my *grandparents'* property. Not my Dad's or the old Lange property. I liked that.

"Okay."

"Mind if I put my guys to work clearing the property now?"

"Yes, please." In fact, it was more than fine by me. It would be easier to keep Will out of it now than when he was feeling better. "Will is improving but far from good, though he won't admit it. I don't want him to risk any additional injury."

"Agreed. And I don't need the liability risk, so I'll be clear about it with him. He'll understand that."

"Keep him healthy, Jim, please. I need him."

"Will do. I understand you have big plans coming up soon."

I smiled at the phone. "Yes, indeed. Did Will tell you?"

"About the wedding? He called me yesterday, but we'd already heard, of course."

"Of course. Word gets around. I apologize for not calling sooner." That was said out of courtesy. Will and I had been engaged less than three days. I continued, "So that's what I wanted to speak with you about. It will be a simple wedding, a quiet celebration here at Wildflower House. I won't be sending out formal invites. The date isn't set yet, but it will be soon. I'm thinking in three weeks, so mid-March. I hope you and Libbie will join us? After all, if not for you, Will and I would never have met. And if not for you being on the scene to help rescue Will . . . things might have gone very differently."

He laughed softly. "That's true, at least regarding your father needing the landscaping work and the two of you meeting."

"Thank you, Jim."

"My pleasure."

After we disconnected, I sat, lost in a strange mix of happy and sad tears, thinking maybe that was the bottom-line truth that I'd missed all along. Maybe it wasn't about cruel fate toying with our lives, but that our lives themselves were tapestries of good and bad, of happy and sad. Balance? Maybe there wasn't one without the other.

If I wanted Will, then I had to take the risk that came with that commitment.

And allow the yarn ball of life to tangle or unroll as it would.

~~~~

I wandered back to the foyer to check on the piano tuner. He was a quiet man with a small, neat beard—a man of apparently few words who was more interested in the piano than in chatting with me. I sensed I was interrupting.

"I'll be in the other room working, so if you need me, just yell or knock on the door. I'm expecting someone else, my fiancé, to arrive anytime now. Other than that, you should be undisturbed."
~~~~

Fiancé . . . how natural that had felt to say. Fiancé.

He nodded, not understanding the importance of that word to me and my world, and went back to tuning the inner workings of the piano.

Shrugging, I left him there. When I entered the workroom, Laura said, "If you've got a few minutes, I'd like to go over what I've found out, and I have a list of suggestions to review with you."

"I'm not expecting Will until later, so this is a good time." He was driving already. Much too soon, in my opinion, but he'd promised to be careful and not overdo. Mostly, he was just driving between his mom's house, his apartment, and Wildflower. He was still in pain but had stopped taking the pain pills altogether. I was amazed that pain seemed different for him than it had for me. Mine had messed with my head too . . . but maybe that had been less the physical pain and more of the emotional pain. Plus, I'd had broken bones. At any rate, it did my heart good to see him steadily improving and his outlook so cheerful.

I sat with Laura, and we reviewed her list. Laura, at first tentative, explained what she'd found out, her recommendations for activities that ranked high in our region, examples of brochures and course offerings from comparable business. My mood sank a little at hearing that, because we were far from being comparable with any of those businesses. Laura noticed. "It's a goal, Kara. Partly aspirational and part action items. We can do this."

Yes, we can, I thought. *We.*

"The website designer is ready to go when you say so. You'd already done the hard work. I pulled it together and fleshed it out. It's decision time. She's just waiting for a few last specifics from you."

She handed me a sheet of paper. "These are my recommendations. Please review them, make changes or not, then I'll communicate with her, if you're comfortable with that? I may not be good at data input and those computer spreadsheets, but one thing I know is computer surfing and online shopping and travel sites." She shrugged. "Not that I've traveled much, but I'm a . . . What do they call it? An armchair tourist?"

I laughed.

"I also love collecting brochures, so I'm enjoying that part of it too. Thank you so much for giving me the chance."

"Don't thank me. I owe more thanks to you than I can say."

"Well, I may have overstepped, actually. You may be annoyed with me. I promise that I haven't suggested any kind of commitment . . . but it's about the Lange property." She stopped and kind of gazed into the air, somewhere beyond me. "It's so odd when I say that name. As if I'm divorced from it. There is a familiarity . . . maybe. Or maybe it's just that I want it to feel familiar." She shrugged. "It doesn't matter. But I know it has negative connections for you."

"Jim Mitchell is starting the clearing this week. Of course, he'll have to do some road improvements and such first, so it won't happen overnight."

"Are you still considering what you'd like to do with the property?"

"Yes."

"During my phone calls, I had lots of conversations, and one thing led to another. I chatted with a woman whose nieces need a place for a stable."

"Horse stable? At one point, we considered something like that, but it's way out of scope for what I'm doing here. Too specialized and too much twenty-four/seven active engagement required. Like running a whole other business. Plus, I know nothing about horses."

"Well, so this is the thing—and again, I didn't say you were thinking about selling that acreage, I promise, but I mentioned Wildflower and Cub Creek and so on, and she was saying her nieces are being evicted from the land where they've been running a stable for several years and need somewhere to move to. They lost their lease due to a new subdivision going in—gosh, they're springing up everywhere, aren't they—so now they must find somewhere else. They've been looking for property that will work but can't afford to outbid the developers."

She stopped speaking so abruptly that I was waiting for her to explain why she was telling me all this, and then I realized she already had.

"Sell the land?" Frankly, I hadn't seriously considered selling it. It was my father's land, where he'd grown up, and it directly adjoined the Wildflower property—though the acres of forest on the Wildflower side guaranteed privacy. Still, selling it would take its use and management beyond my control. I felt my heart rate speeding up.

"I'm sorry if I messed up. I've gone beyond what you

asked of me, haven't I?"

"Actually, I don't think you have." It cost me to say that, and it cost me more to add, "Tell me why you think it's a good idea." I tried to keep my expression clear.

"About the stables? Well, they must move. No choice about that. They have a little time to make that happen, but not much. And this isn't a big operation. They board horses, offer riding lessons, but also . . . and this is the thing that grabbed my heart and proves I'm not a good businesswoman, Kara. I accept that." She sniffled and dabbed at her lashes with a tissue. "They have a therapy riding program. I investigated it, and it's a real thing. It's run by two sisters—actual sisters, I mean—and they work with individuals and programs to introduce children and young adults with physical or emotional problems to horses and riding. It's a bona fide therapy. Amanda Brewster, the woman I was talking to about supplies we'll need for our own classes, knows about the program because her grandson benefits from the therapy. The program will end if the sisters can't find a place to move to—a property that's suitable and that they can afford."

"Thank you for the good work," I said. "I'll take a look at your notes, though I'm guessing your research is sound."

I took the folder. "As for the property . . . I'll think about it." I heard Victoria's voice in my head saying not to get in my own way. I must've cracked a small smile, because Laura smiled and seemed to ease her posture a tad. "Laura, I'm very impressed by what you've gathered. Never, ever feel intimidated by me or my . . . manner.

That's my problem. Not yours."

"I know your heart, Kara."

"Laura. Dear Aunt Laura." I reached across the table and took her hand. "I spoke with Lewis. He plans to attend the wedding. His daughter will come with him if she can get off work."

She clapped her hands. "Oh, how wonderful. That will be so perfect. Never in a million years did I ever think I'd have all this . . . this family in my life."

"I feel the same. A year ago . . . So much has changed since then. I'm still getting used to having extended family, and friends that are like family." I paused to breathe and gather my thoughts. "I called Lewis because I wanted to give him a heads-up. I thought I was going to ask him to give me away . . . but I didn't."

"Why not?"

"I realized that it was all wrong. I'll get to know him better, and I'd like for him to be there with us at the ceremony . . . but I hope you'll agree to give me away. To stand with me as . . . in place of my parent."

She was flustered. Her cheeks flushed. She waved her hands, but only in a brief flurry. She jumped up from her chair and came to me, taking my hands and speaking straight to my heart. "Yes, I'll be proud to stand with you and 'give you away,' but just know that I'm not actually giving you away. I've only just found you. You're stuck with me, dear Kara."

Seemed like there was a lot of hugging happening these days, and it happened again now. Hugging and crying too, but with happy tears.

Soon after, I went to the kitchen to fix us a snack. Mostly, I needed fresh air. I took the joy with me, holding it close and thinking of my parents. Of my father.

Of my mother. I remembered the items my father had saved. There wasn't much. A few old photos, which I treasured, but also there'd been a white dress in a bag. I didn't fool myself that it would be suitable to wear after all these years and stored as it was. Might not want to anyway. Their marriage hadn't been a happy union. But maybe a snippet of fabric sewn in some way that could be carried or worn discreetly . . . I didn't want to draw curious questions about it, or I might get weepy all over again.

Forgetting that I'd intended to fetch iced tea for us, I stood there, staring out the window. The sun was bright. The day was cold, but not frigid, and there was no wind. I went to the kitchen door, opened it partway, and let the freshness hit my hot face. I closed my eyes and breathed in deeply, releasing the breath slowly, and as I did, I heard music.

A few random notes at first. Then more, and it became a tune.

The piano tuner must be checking his work.

And then the tune became "Simple Gifts."

I froze. Unable to breathe, once again seeing before me the brilliance of the sunlit wildflower field, but this time seeing myself distantly, walking in the midst of the flowers, and my father and Nicole standing on the porch and calling me to come in and tour the house. I was seeing them from behind, almost close enough for me to touch.

My father's arm was near Nicole's, his fingers were touching hers, but even that tiny gesture of intimacy was discreetly camouflaged by the railing.

My lungs hurt. I forced air into them, still hearing the music, but stronger now, "Simple Gifts," perhaps not as Elder Brackett had intended, and not as Copland had incorporated it into his own composition, but softer and yet wilder all at the same time. It pulled at my heart and pushed at my lungs. I closed my eyes against the pain and held to the doorframe lest I fall.

He must stop playing. He must. I could not bear it.

I pushed away from the doorframe. On shaky legs, I hurried through the kitchen. Laura was standing in the hallway, staring toward the piano. Beyond her, I could see the tuner at the front door facing this way, a tool of some sort dangling from his hand as if forgotten. The piano was hidden from me, the corner not visible from this angle, so I moved faster, nearly frantic to get there—not to stop the music but to reach it before it *did* stop.

Will was seated at the piano. The notes thrummed in my head as if sent directly from his fingers. I stood, now immobile.

When the crescendo had been reached and as the last note died away, he lifted his fingers from the keys. He held them suspended above the keys for a few seconds, and then he looked at the tuner and said, "Sounds good."

I'd never told him about the music I'd heard the day I first saw Wildflower. I knew I hadn't. No one knew of it but me.

"Will . . ."

The sheet music was in front of him. But he'd departed from it as written—far outside of how the notes had been scored.

"Why that song?" I asked, my voice rough.

He said, "It was in the bench with the rest of the music. On top."

Of course it was.

"Will . . ."

It was only the two of us here. I'd forgotten the others—had ceased to see them. Until the tuner spoke.

"Man, that was something. Most test the piano after the tuning. Some are excellent players. Some I'd even call pianists. But I've rarely heard anything like that." He shook his head, his voice dropping almost to a mutter. "And never on one of these vintage uprights."

Still talking, he resumed gathering his gear and packing it into a case. "If you're ever performing anywhere in the area, please let me know. I'd love to be there to hear it." With that, he put his card on top of the piano, along with an invoice. "Almost hate to charge you for the trip, Ms. Hart."

He shook his head. "No, not really. But still, it was a rare pleasure. This piano was in pretty good shape, and a Steinway has a special sound, truly, but with playing like that, you might consider having an expert restorer in to check the parts. Do a little reconditioning. I've jotted a name and number of one you can absolutely trust on the back of my card." He picked up his work bag. "Let me know when it's time to tune it again. I'd suggest six months, given your fiancé's technique."

And he left.

Laura said, almost bursting with questions, "My goodness, Will. Where'd you learn to play like that?"

"My grandmother. She was a pianist and going places, as I understand it, until she gave it up and came home to her parents, married and so on. She taught me to play . . . though, she was often exasperated because I could read music, but I just couldn't stay with it as written." He grinned. "Always wanted to color out of the lines and fill in the blank spaces."

"Will. That was amazing," I said.

"I'm out of practice."

"No more. You will play for me regularly. Please."

He shook his head. "I play if I enjoy playing. I'd rather be outside planting. I think she was disappointed in me because of that."

It was so strange to see this tall, well-built man who was so good with growing and building things looking slightly downcast.

"No," I said. "I'm quite certain she was never disappointed in you."

"Think so?" He nodded. "That's her ring you're wearing."

My eyes stung again. Crying with Laura a short time ago, now ready to cry with Will. Instead, I reached out to him, and he half rose, then stopped and groaned. He had to catch his breath, and it hurt me to watch him in pain. Finally, he said, "It's not so bad when I'm standing or sitting. It's the in-between that's a killer."

I couldn't help myself. Simply couldn't resist. I

smiled and said, "No more in-between for us, Will Mercer, and no coloring between the lines either. We'll find our own way."

He'd eased himself back down to the bench. He looked at me and said, "Together. I'll follow you anywhere, Kara Hart."

"Follow me to the kitchen first? Let's have a snack, and you can take it easy."

"I'll eat my snack standing, if you don't mind. Might even take a slow walk down to the creek. I'd like some air and sun."

"To the creek it is, then."

~~~~

Will and I left via the back door and strolled over to the garden area. I held Will's hand and felt his music still with us. Around us. A strange wordless duet between Will's version of "Simple Gifts" and Copland's *Appalachian Spring* . . . but soft, almost distant, in my head. It was a lovely accompaniment as we walked, even as the threads of it faded away.

We stopped in front of the statue of the girl reaching out to touch butterflies. Dad's marker was before us, at the base of the statue.

"Thank you, Will."

"You're welcome." He looked at me. "For what, specifically?"

"For the music. For the parlor bookcase. For burying my father. The list is almost endless." I met his eyes. "And
~~~~

growing."

"It's early days, Kara. I meant it when I said we could do amazing things together."

In the sunshine, and with no breeze, the air was pleasant, if not actually warm. Around us the first row of azaleas, the smaller, early spring bloomers, were dotted with pink buds. We held hands, each thinking our own thoughts, until I said, "Can we walk down to the bench? It's been a while since I sat there."

So we did. The sound of the creek flowing by melded with the bird calls in the woods on either side and across on the far side of the water. Will lowered himself slowly to the seat, and I stayed on his good side so that I could move up close, body to body, warmth to warmth, and put my head on his shoulder.

I sighed.

"What's wrong, Kara?"

"Nothing. Not even one little thing. This moment is so perfect. I wish I could bottle it. Keep it. Protect it. Maybe never move forward."

He released my hand and eased his arm from between us to put it across my shoulders, to caress my hair and squeeze my shoulder.

"We'd miss so much," he said. "Including the wedding."

I smiled. "Yes, that's true. I worry, though. Maybe it's too perfect."

He laughed softly. "Can you handle the stress of perfection? You're running out of time to back out."

"Not a chance of me backing out. Too many guests

are depending upon us to make an appearance."

"Very responsible of you to consider them."

"I invited Jim and Libbie to the wedding."

His face lit up. "I'm glad. They aren't technically family, but Jim's been good to me. More than an employer, especially after my father died. I'd like to ask him to stand with me as best man."

"Excellent," I said. "If there's anyone else who's important to you, Will, important to be there on our big day, tell me. We're already beyond *small and private.* And . . . there's something else."

"I'm listening."

"Jim is going to clear the property. He has promised me you won't help. At all. I want you to promise me that too."

"Kara . . . listen, sometimes my job comes with risks . . ."

"Not in this case. He's starting this week, and you are still healing. With the wedding so soon, I won't risk additional injuries, or anything that might slow down your recovery."

"I'll meet you at the altar, regardless of how I have to get there." He stared at me for a moment before saying, "I promise."

"Thank you," I said.

After a quiet moment, I added, "I told Jim that, if not for him, we never would've met."

He made a soft noise. I waited to hear what he was about to say.

"Maybe. I like to think that we were destined to meet.

That if it hadn't happened as it did, with Jim and your father talking business, then it would've happened some other way. I think that you, the essential you, are my lodestone. My talisman. Don't laugh at me."

"Never. I'll never laugh when you use words like that."

"I think I knew you existed for me before I ever met you. I told you that I fell for you the moment I saw you. But it was more than that. I knew it was you—the one I was expecting. Seth got in the way for a while." Will shrugged as he tried to laugh, but it hurt him. After taking a second to breathe, he added, "I worried that I was the only one who understood we were destined for each other, but you figured it out, thank goodness." He kissed me on the temple. "Thank you."

"Laura mentioned something to me that I want to share with you. Get your thoughts on it. It's about the Lange property."

"Yes?"

"She told me about two sisters who run a small horse operation. Boarding horses, riding lessons, but also some therapy work with people who have medical issues or emotional disabilities, who benefit from it. They work on a thin profit margin, and they're losing the lease for the property they are currently on."

Will shifted to see my face. "You're thinking of selling them the land?"

"No. Yes. Oh, maybe. I don't know." I shrugged, leaning even closer to him. "I think I'd like to know more about the business and the owners. I don't want to sell only to have them change their minds about the use and build condos or something. I love the therapy aspect, as well as the small business aspect. In fact, we could maybe work out a deal that provides some access to Wildflower guests, should that ever become a thing." I laughed a little at that.

"I think I know those gals. Can't be too many sister teams around who manage a stable. They work with rescues, too, and offer therapy rides. Britt visited them during her recovery. It helped her. They are legit, as far as I know. Of course, no one—including them—can guarantee the success of a business. I suppose you could lease them the land with restrictions. That might help their bottom line. On the other hand, it might open you up to liability issues. Might be one more thing you'd feel like you have to manage."

"You are smart, Will Mercer."

"You are smarter, Kara Hart. Soon to be Mercer."

"Kara Mercer." I made my own satisfied noise. "I like the sound of that." After a pause, I said, "So I was thinking about Dad and it being his property. I'm thinking he might approve of this solution."

"No doubt about it. But it's your choice, Kara. Not mine. Not your father's." He cleared his throat. "One thing we haven't discussed is a prenup. I'm bringing willingness and love to the marriage, but you have the property. Valuable property."

"Or a money pit."

"No, the land alone is worth a small fortune. But that aside, my uncle is an attorney, and I've asked him to draw up a document making it clear that Wildflower House and the land is yours, apart from any marital property we may acquire."

I must've made a disapproving noise because Will tightened his arm around me.

"I'm happy for anyone to say that I married above me. I am, for sure, though I like to think I bring a certain—I don't know—maybe *flair* to the union?"

"Flair?"

"Why not? Flair is good. But that being said, I won't have anyone whispering that it was for your assets. You'll sign it? Promise me."

Instead, I kissed him. When I was done, I said, "I have one more request."

"What's that?"

"Will you play the piano for me regularly?"

"Seriously?"

"Yes. Absolutely."

"Then you've got it. I promise."

"And one day, I'm going to tell you a story about a woman who found herself in a field of wildflowers and heard a song, and whose life changed beyond all recognition."

"Tell me now."

I smiled. "No, it's a *someday* story. Along with another story about a woman waiting alone, in an empty room, for a man who loves her to dance with her."

"Okay, now *that* one I can handle. I'll help you write the ending to that story myself, in person, anytime you're ready."

~~~~

A few days later, the day the actual clearing of the old Lange property was to start, Will insisted on watching. I insisted we go together. We agreed to travel there by way of the creek path. The creek path was nice and level and didn't involve bending to climb in and out of vehicles.

When we reached the site, Jim waved, but indicated we should stay back, that he'd come over to speak with us. When he did, he brought a small bucket with him.

"I had the guys go over the area with a metal detector in case we found any family items. We're continue keeping an eye out, but there's not much. Textiles and soft items don't last, of course. There's a lot of broken glass and rusty cans. We did find some small odds and ends. I haven't rinsed them yet. Do you want to take them with you now?"

He was offering the bucket to me. There were small items, mud-covered. A small chain, maybe. A coin or button. But one was larger than the rest. I picked it up despite the grime.

"What's this?" It was rounded and smooth, with a white, flattish surface that felt glassy. A squarish hole was in the back. I turned it over in my hand. "A doorknob?"

"Yes, porcelain. Had to come from a door in the house. Maybe we'll find more of them."

"Oh." I was thinking of the hands that had touched this. Had felt this same surface beneath their flesh. "Thank you, Jim."

He gestured toward a couple of his workers who
~~~~

brought plastic paint buckets from one of the trucks. They upended them for seats. For us.

Will sat gingerly, carefully. Jim asked him if he was okay.

"Yeah. Getting better every day. Have a wedding coming up."

Jim looked amused. *Guys,* I thought. At least Jim seemed as determined as I was to keep Will from engaging with the work. I was grateful for that.

"How's the wedding planning coming along?"

I said, "Sort of like a snowball rolling downhill. Growing bigger all the time."

Jim laughed. "Good for the both of you. Libbie says to let her know if you need any help."

As Jim walked back to the work area, we noticed two women standing off to the side. They must've hiked in from the main road. My first thought was that they were connected to the work being done, and I suppose in a way they were, but more particularly with the outcome. When they spotted us sitting on our buckets, one turned to leave but the other grabbed her arm, nodded toward us, and insisted they both move forward.

Two blonde women—I guessed them to be in their late twenties. They wore jeans and jackets and work boots that looked almost as serious as Will's.

"Will," I said. He was staring at the work being done. I said his name again and then pointed. "Is that them?"

"Yes, I think so."

I saw him tensing at the idea of standing. "Stay seated. They know about your accident. Everyone does." I stood as they approached.

"Hello. I'm Kara Hart. I think you know Will? At least, you know his sister, Britt?"

They nodded.

"I'm surprised to see you here."

"Yes." The taller sister spoke first. "Apologies. We weren't trying to intrude. We were just hoping to get a look at the land."

The shorter sister, who I guessed was also the younger, broke in. "You know we're losing our lease?" She added, "We'd like to talk to you about buying or leasing the property."

The first sister said, "Sorry, she's anxious. We have to move in a few months. Even if we can find land we can afford, it will cost to get it set up, prepped, and we need a barn and a house. We have some resources, and nearby is best for us, but land has gotten expensive in this area."

Just at that moment, the front loader was raising a chunk of roof and the old house frame shuddered, then metal screamed against metal as it caved in. We all jumped.

As my heart settled back into its normal rhythm, I said, "Come see me after the wedding. Not *right* after the wedding." Given their earnestness, it seemed important to add that part.

"Give me a number and either I or my aunt, Laura, will set up a meeting. Understand, I'm not against the idea, but I also don't want to sell it just to sell it. I want it used for a worthwhile purpose or not at all, so please come prepared to convince me."

"We will. We'll be ready."

They walked away, talking low. One of them elbowed the other, but in a good-natured way. Very sisterly, I thought. They looked upbeat.

I sat down again, saying, "I hope I won't have to disappoint them."

"Hey, you're giving them a hearing. A chance. You're a businesswoman. They are also businesswomen. It's up to them to make the best pitch they can."

"My dad would've said something very much like that. Sometimes, though, there's more to it than numbers."

"The heart of the matter?" Will smiled and took my hand.

"Indeed."

Together we sat in companionable silence and watched the dismantling of my father's childhood home, and the place where I'd almost lost my true love.

I squeezed his hand. "Are things moving too fast or not fast enough?"

"I started to say not fast enough, but just at this moment, Kara, it feels like it's moving along just about perfectly."

CHAPTER TEN

March, a week before the wedding ~

Plans for the wedding ceremony had expanded to include a reception after. Like a small party, I was told. Which made sense. After all, we'd have cake, right? We wanted people to eat it. Both Victoria and Laura supported this idea.

"Yes," I said. "Why not?"

Victoria did as she'd promised. She talked with all the primary persons involved, took down the details, and went to work with the help of her minions, Nicole and Aunt Laura. The output was a wondrous, slightly mystical combination of my wishes and her choices. Almost miraculously, Maddie Lyn had a dress. Her *bride dress* she called it. She spun and showed off the white silk skirt with a netting overlay and a colorful sash handstitched with wildflowers. She had a white basket that would be filled with petals on the big day. Victoria and Laura had worked together on outfitting Maddie and on finding their own dresses. It was a pale yellow for Laura and pale blue for Victoria. Nicole declined to be an attendant because she wanted to be close at hand for her mother and for Maddie too. As for me, I insisted that my dress be simple and not necessarily full-length. Victoria dragged me out on an all-day shopping expedition, and a little more of that magic did its work and I found one that I liked—an ankle-length sheath in a soft ivory color with ivory embroidery and fine lace and seed pearls across the bodice. It required very little adjustment, of course. I was happy—and even happier that Victoria was handling the details and coordination.

A week before the wedding, Sue Deale came knocking. I hadn't seen her since the day she brought the potato soup and bread, but of course, as the guest list grew, I'd included her and her husband. Today, Mr. Deale was sitting in his truck out front while Sue was knocking on my door. I was surprised that she hadn't just walked in.

"Hi, Sue. You're a week early," I said, joking.

"Here's the bride. You couldn't be any more beautiful than you already are. I think you and Will make the perfect couple."

She was holding a large bag. Like a fancy gift bag. A wedding gift?

"I brought something for you. I only just realized I had it a few days ago, and then I was frantic I might not be able to put my hands on it because it was stored among all those things I have from my cousin Mary."

She grinned. "Mary was a collector of things—of too many things, some say—and I guess I am too." She walked over to the foyer table but set the bag on the floor. She reached down into the bag, saying, "But I found it, and while I was looking, I found this too." She straightened, but slowly, and I took her arm in reflex. "Old and stiff, that's me. If you live long enough, old age will catch up with you every time."

I didn't know what to say to that and figured she wasn't expecting a response because now she was focused on a thin box. Wide-ish and longish and old. She lifted the lid, and I saw a large photograph—a faded copy of the photo that was hanging on the wall above the foyer table.

"Yes, it's the same. Can't imagine why Mary would have a copy, much less two copies, but this was in one of the boxes I took from the attic when I cleared the house, so it may not have even been hers."

She held it up near the other photo. "Do you see?"

It was fun and all that, quite a surprise, maybe, but I didn't understand her obvious delight. This was the same photo, but never protected by a frame like the one I already had, so it was in less-than-perfect condition.

"Well? Do you see?"

"I'm sorry, Sue, but I don't understand."

"Here. Wait." She fished her phone out of her coat pocket. It was one of the latest cell phones. That surprised me, though it shouldn't have. One just never knew about people. It was never smart to judge people by their covers.

Sue found the flashlight app on her phone, and holding the photo with one hand, she beamed the light on the photo, focusing on the area of the skirts of the young girls in the front row.

The light did glint on something. I squinted. Was that writing? Maybe old pencil markings?

"What does it say, Sue?"

"A name. Focus, Kara. Get your eyeglasses if you need to. Oh, wait." She handed me the photo and began digging in her purse again. This time her hand emerged with a magnifying glass. But by then, I'd already seen it. The faint lines had become cursive letters, and the letters formed words.

"Names?"

"Yes. Remember that day we were saying how much fun it would be to identify them?" She frowned. "I think we said it . . . At any rate, I had that discussion with someone. So now we can."

I stared along with Sue, then said, "Wait." I called out Laura's name. She was in the workroom with the door closed, but she heard me and came rushing out.

"What's wrong?"

Heavens above. Seemed like everyone was always asking me what was wrong. I was going to have to reexamine my communication skills.

"Stand here beside me."

"Hi, Sue," Laura said as she joined us. "Oh, another photo. Oh, my. It's the same photo, isn't it?"

"Sue found it. It has names." I held the photo in one hand and pointed to the girl in the front row near the middle.

Sue pointed at a child in the front row, keeping the light steady on the writing.

I said, "It says Laura Powell."

"Of course. Your Laura who married Mr. Lange was her daughter."

Words deserted me.

Laura made a funny noise, and I looked at her. She needed a chair. I took her arm and pushed her toward the piano bench.

"Are you okay?"

She said, "Oh. My. My grandmother? Is that what you're saying, Sue?"

Sue said, "Indeed. Though I don't know why you're so surprised. All these folks have been in this general area for generations." She fanned Laura with the photograph as she said, "I found it while I was looking for something else, something special. But before we get to that, let's look again. Look at the girl next to Laura. The one with the brown curls."

Laura squinted, and Sue directed her light on that area. But I'd already seen it. Mercer. Samantha Mercer.

I sat down beside her.

Sue said, "It could be a coincidence. I'm sure about Laura Powell, but not about the Mercer girl. It will be easy enough to find out. Vivian will know."

The photograph was back in my hands. I'd imagined these girls and women posing on the front porch of this house near the turn of the last century. Their lives and their choices had been somewhat different. But their hearts had felt every bit as much hope and joy and sorrow. How different were we, really?

"I admit I'm stunned, Sue. Seems like bits and pieces of Wildflower House, from before it was Wildflower House, keep finding their way back here."

Sue laughed. "Mr. Deale would certainly be delighted

if more of it would!" She clapped her hands. "But wait, I have the main thing in the bag. The thing I was actually looking for."

As she reached back into the bag, she said, "You know that Mary had no children." She laughed, as only Sue could do. "It was seriously out of style when my sons got married, and their brides had different tastes, but it's been out of style long enough to be *in* style again. Vintage, as they say." She drew out another box, smaller. "It's a shame, really. The veil was ruined by being left in the attic for too many decades. But"—she paused to stare at me—"I don't really see you in a veil. Are you planning to wear one?"

"No."

"Well, this, with your features, your high cheekbones and hazel eyes . . . you could pull this off beautifully."

She handed me the box, and I opened it. The box was old. There was an old jeweler's label still clinging to the back. I stared. A tiara? No, not a tiara.

Sue said, "Art deco? Flapper style? Not quite sure, but it's exquisite, isn't it? The thin silver band is so delicate. It goes across your forehead"—she touched her own—"just so. And then the comb with that intricate filigree design comes around to secure it by slipping into your hair." She removed it from the box. "Hold still." I did, and she held it in place, taking my hand to hold the comb part stable. "You have to wear your hair up to make it work."

We moved to the mirror as a strange sort of three-person unit holding the glittering headpiece in place. Laura was beaming as we looked into the mirror over the fireplace.

It was stunning, even despite the awkwardness of the hands holding it.

Behind me, Sue said, “Mary and Rob lived an amazing love story, including their many years here at this house. But no daughter. No child to pass this on to. It can be your *something borrowed* as you and Will continue to grow your own amazing love story.”

Chapter Eleven

~ A wedding event at Wildflower House ~

In the end, I didn't descend the grand stairs as Victoria had envisioned for the wedding, but only used them to reach the main floor as I'd done every day for almost a year. In future days, I was certain *other* brides would someday in the future, but not me.

Only a few white folding chairs festooned with ribbons and baby's breath remained in the sitting room. They'd been intended for guests but were unneeded, after all.

The rooms seemed empty because most of the furniture had been moved out in anticipation of the ceremony that was to take place in the parlor and now would not. Only the dining room was the same. Or almost the same, because in the middle of the table was an honest-to-goodness tiered cake with buttercream icing, and the top edge of each layer was decorated with colorful wildflowers.

If the rooms were otherwise empty of well-wishers, still there was no mistaking the love that filled the tall rooms and wide hallways. And the heart of Wildflower House was here. And the heart was also outside. It beat in me and in the guests waiting in the garden with Will—perhaps even in those who came before or would come after us, because the heart of Wildflower House would always be wherever love reigned.

I'd found a home here—and a business—had lost my father and gained a fiancé. And today—this glorious day in March—was our wedding day.

Spring was in the air for sure, as it should be. The grass was greening up, and the redbud trees had leafed out. There were fewer wildflowers blooming on the grounds than there'd been a year ago, but the day, and the weather, was a gift we simply couldn't overlook. Our friends had moved most of the chairs outside as they went, and my dearly loved friends in my bridal party had rearranged the bride's route.

I joined Maddie Lyn in the narrow hallway between the project workroom and the grand stairs. The plan was for us to walk straight out the side door to the small porch, and from there around the house to the garden. Maddie looked very serious. It was unlike her.

"Are you all right? You look lovely. That dress is perfect."

She whispered so low I couldn't hear.

"What did you say, sweetheart?"

"My feet. The shoes hurt my feet."

I started to say she wouldn't have to wear them for long, but then . . . it occurred to me that hearts did reign here, and as Kara Hart, queen for the day, I opened the stairway door and said, "Have a seat."

She looked afraid, but only briefly. She worried about the attic sometimes. But then she did as I asked. I stooped, trying not to muss my dress, and she held up one foot. I slipped the shoe off. Yes, the shoe had dug deep lines around the top of her foot—obvious despite the white tights she was wearing.

"I have a solution."

A single tear was suspended on her lashes. I touched it to take it away.

"Let's ditch the shoes. Do you mind walking in the grass in your bare feet? The stone walkway might be chilly."

"Barefoot? No shoes?"

"No shoes."

She wasted no time in kicking off the other shoe, then hiked up her long skirt and began hastily pulling off the tights.

I smiled, saying, "Let me help you so you don't tear them."

A huge *whew* of relief from Maddie Lyn confirmed my decision.

What would Nicole think? It didn't matter. At least there'd be no grass stains on the tights. Nicole was outside assisting her mother, Mel. By the time she saw the pink tootsies peeking out from under the hem of Maddie Lyn's dress, it would be too late. I suspected she'd privately agree with my decision anyway.

Victoria was suddenly there in the hallway beside me, slightly breathless and handing me the bouquet.

"Everyone is in place now. I've never seen such an exodus en masse. It was wonderful!"

She pressed my hands around the bouquet, then released them slowly. She tugged at my sleeve, at a bit of lace near my throat, and then did an almost-touch of my hair before pronouncing it "perfect" and stepping back.

We'd put my hair up as Sue had suggested. It looked lovely with the hairpiece she'd loaned me. Privately, I cared less about the perfection of the hair and more about tonight when Will would remove the pins, release my hair, and run his hands through it. And that anticipated moment had no feel of fate or chance, but of destiny. That despite the fear, the worries, the angst—the past and the unknown future—inevitable or not, we had found each other and a path we could travel together.

There might even have been a bit of coincidence in it. Though sometimes I wondered if people often followed paths they didn't recognize as already set, and whether choices were always choices. But I didn't have time to think about all that because I had a wedding to attend. *Mine.*

I would not borrow trouble. For today, at least, I would embrace happiness one moment, one day, at a time. Maybe it would even become a habit. I patted the bit of satin and lace I'd pinned inside the bodice of my dress over my heart. Just a little something from my mother's gown. A remembrance of her on this special day. My future would be different from hers, and I knew she was cheering.

The door to the side porch opened. Nicole looked in.

"Ready?" she asked.

Laura was there beside her. She stepped inside. "Ready?" she asked me, echoing Nicole's question.

"In my whole life, I've never been *more* ready."

Nicole laughed.

Laura said, "Then let's step out to the porch and get on with the ceremony before a sudden spring storm blows in. You never can tell around here."

I almost said, "It wouldn't dare," but I didn't, because really there was no point in tempting fate. "Let's go," I said. I whispered to Laura, "You look lovely, Aunt Laura. Thank you for standing in for Dad, and my mom too."

We left the porch and stepped onto the path that would lead us around to the backyard.

Nicole scooted ahead to claim her seat. Maddie followed but more sedately, as she'd been instructed, carefully dropping flower petals one by one. Victoria preceded us, and gone was the over-the-top woman who often frustrated me. Her walk, her movement, was . . . regal.

With Laura's arm in mine, we rounded the corner, and there before me was a host of people. Faces smiling. Some eyes were sparkling with mostly unshed tears. The good will and love were palpable. Mel and Nicole were seated up front, as were Vivian and Britt. Sue and her husband, the book club gals and guy, many members of the Ladies' Auxiliary, Uncle Lewis—yes, he was here too, with his daughter, Laura. Will's extended family, some of whom I remembered from the New Year's get-together, were here, too. I saw Libbie. Dan was sitting near her. Moore

Blackwell and his wife, Stacy. So many others. And toward the back, almost hidden by those in front, was Seth.

Our guests, some sitting, some standing, were arrayed around the medallion garden with the early spring azaleas in bloom and pots of colorful flowers interspersed around the statue—with Dad's urn interred below.

At that thought, I almost stumbled. Laura sensed it and tightened her arm in mine, but I was confident no one else noticed because I also saw Will waiting for me, flanked by Jim and the pastor, and I knew all was well.

The wildflowers were not yet in full bloom, but I saw the same joy and light in each of these human faces as I'd experienced a year ago when in the midst of that colorful, lovely profusion. This time, there was no music because of the fast move outside, and there was not even a thread of imagined or remembered music in the air—or in my head—but there was birdsong and squirrel chatter and the bright buzz of energy that only love greatly multiplied can create.

It truly was a matter of the heart.

And my heart was complete.

EPILOGUE

~ A wildflower dance ~

As we'd expected, the guests asked about our honeymoon plans. Will and I were vague and noncommittal. We had privately agreed that there was no better place to spend our honeymoon than where we already were—*Wildflower House.* In fact, we'd claimed the best accommodations in the house, the recently renovated large front room with the private bath. *Thanks for the suggestion, Victoria.*

We let everyone think we did have big honeymoon plans—but *secret.*

After the photos were taken and the cake was eaten and the punch bowl was almost empty, Will and I were full to overflowing with good wishes and hugs. We stood together on the front porch, bidding farewell to the last of our wedding guests.

Laura was the very last to leave. She alone knew we were staying here. As she gave me a parting hug, she whispered in my ear, "I'll keep your secret, dear, but be sure to lock the door. You never know who'll walk in."

I laughed and thanked her for the reminder about the

doors at Wildflower House.

As she drove away, I realized I was alone on the porch. Will was gone.

For a long moment, I stood there, only me, lost in a haze of unreality. It was an odd sort of sensation, as if the day—and all that had happened in it—was no more than an illusion.

And then I heard the music.

It was a tune I'd never heard before. In fact, there were two different melodies. One came from the piano, the other . . . not. It had more of a background sound. The tunes overlaid each other, entwining—not truly blending, but complementary.

I approached the front door and paused. Will was seated at the piano, still in his wedding attire, except for his dark suit jacket, which was hung over the newel post.

This music was a special gift meant for me.

Eagerly, I crossed the threshold into the foyer and stood there, waiting, as I watched Will's hands move surely, deftly across the keys. I listened until, too soon, he stopped. Then, as lilting music continued to play from his phone, he stood and walked toward me.

He extended his hand, and I reached out to touch his fingers. Our hands folded around each other.

"Kara Mercer, may I have this dance?"

"Always, Will Mercer."

He slid his arms around me, and in the wide foyer of Wildflower House, we danced.

If there were shadows lurking anywhere, I didn't see them. This moment—this *now*—was what mattered.

As for the two of us—Will believed we would make an amazing team. I was inclined to agree. And regardless and whatever the future brought, we would live it together.

THE END

Thank you for reading *Wildflower Wedding*. I hope you enjoyed it, and all of THE WILDFLOWER HOUSE Series.

Acknowledgments

My sincere thanks to everyone who helped and contributed to The Wildflower House series (*Wildflower Heart* and *Wildflower Hope*) which began with Lake Union Publishing and was continued beyond that in *Wildflower Christmas* and *Wildflower Wedding*, and my gratitude to every reader who had spent time at Wildflower House with Kara and all the characters there. Your encouragement is valued beyond measure.

QUESTIONS FOR DISCUSSION

1. *Wildflower Wedding* deals with the fears that tend to follow us, that we carry inside us, even unacknowledged, and their influence on our choices. This is common to all of us and can even be valuable so long as it doesn't rule us and hold us back from what we should do or should be open to. What fears did you see in Kara and the other characters? What do you notice in other people that they, themselves, may not recognize?

2. Kara changed over the course of the Wildflower House books—for instance, she recognized the learned behavior of fitting herself and her actions into limitations set by others, and tried to change. Victoria also seemed to change over the course of the Wildflower House books, but did she? Or was it that Kara's view of her friend changed after she, Kara, was able to cast off the hurt and anger, and see Victoria more objectively?

3. Nicole said that Kara and Will meshed well. As the author, it seemed to me that they provided traits and strengths that the other lacked—and that supported the other and encouraged the things that made them stronger and more positive. How do you think their personalities meshed?

AUTHOR'S NOTE

This book is set to release in February 2022. It was impossible to write fiction in 2021 and not be constantly reminded of the changes we've all experienced during the time of the virus, of how hospital stays and visits became so difficult, the risks of gatherings, the damage to small businesses and loved ones lost . . . so many changes in our lives that we could never have imagined. But I chose *not* to write a story about the virus. *Wildflower Wedding* picks up where the preceding Wildflower House stories left off—before the virus and the situation we've all been dealing with for the past two-plus years. As with books one through three, I'd like *Wildflower Wedding* also to be a story of happiness and hope because whatever the future brings, and whatever differences exist, we are on this path together and the journey matters.

~ Grace Greene, January 2022

Books by Grace Greene

Emerald Isle, North Carolina Series

Beach Rental *(Book 1)*

Beach Winds *(Book 2)*

Beach Wedding *(Book 3)*

"Beach Towel" (A Short Story)

Beach Walk *(Christmas Novella)*

Barefoot Tides Two-Book Series

A Barefoot Tide *(Book 1)*

A Dancing Tide *(Book 2)*

Beach Single-Title Novellas

Beach Christmas *(Christmas Novella)*

Clair *(Beach Brides Novella Series)*

Cub Creek Novels ~ Series and Single Titles

Cub Creek *(Cub Creek Series, Book 1)*

Leaving Cub Creek *(Cub Creek Series, Book 2)*

The Happiness In Between

The Memory of Butterflies

A Light Last Seen

The Wildflower House Novels

Wildflower Heart *(Book 1)*

Wildflower Hope *(Book 2)*

Wildflower Christmas *(A Wildflower House Novella) (Bk 3)*

Wildflower Wedding *(A Wildflower House Novella) (Bk 4)*

Virginia Country Roads

Kincaid's Hope

A Stranger in Wynnedower

www.GraceGreene.com

About the Author

Photo © 2018 Amy G Photography

Grace Greene is an award-winning and USA Today bestselling author of women's fiction set in the countryside of her native Virginia *(The Happiness In Between, The Memory of Butterflies, the Cub Creek Series, and The Wildflower House Series)* and on the breezy beaches of Emerald Isle, North Carolina *(The Emerald Isle, NC Stories Series, and Barefoot Tides Series)*. Her debut novel, *Beach Rental*, and the sequel, *Beach Winds*, were both Top Picks by RT Book Reviews magazine. The release of *A Barefoot Tide*, represented the merging of two worlds—that of Cub Creek and Emerald Isle, through the eyes of a new character, and continues in the sequel, *A Dancing Tide* released in October 2021. In February 2022, *Wildflower Wedding* joined *The Wildflower House Series* lineup.

Visit www.gracegreene.com for more information and to connect with Grace.

Made in the USA
Middletown, DE
23 December 2022

20281852R00109